"I can't bear it.

"You treat it so lightly, as though it's nothing, but how do you think I'll feel when I know you're out there, suspended in space? Stephen, how can you put me through this?"

"It's the way I live. I'm made to walk the wire."

"I don't think I could have a future with a man who walks the wire," murmured Julie, looking down at the floor.

He tipped a finger beneath her chin and forced her eyes to meet his. "But you care, don't you? Admit it, Juliana! You care for me as I care for you." His eyes cut into her like chips of blue glass. His reverent hand stroked her hair; his arm pulled her close. He bent his head until their lips touched, and then she was clasping him to her as though she would never, ever let him go...."

D0680890

ABOUT THE AUTHOR

"As soon as I saw the magnificent Tallulah Gorge and learned that two high-wire artists had walked across it, I knew I had to weave a story around this special place," says Pamela Browning. *To Touch the Stars* is that story.

Pam enjoys researching her books almost as much as she loves writing them. For *To Touch the Stars*, she interviewed circus performers, went to the circus, gaped at Tallulah Gorge and ate lots of goulash.

Books by Pamela Browning

HARLEQUIN AMERICAN ROMANCE

101—CHERISHED BEGINNINGS
116—HANDYMAN SPECIAL
123—THROUGH EYES OF LOVE
131—INTERIOR DESIGNS
140—EVER SINCE EVE
150—FOREVER IS A LONG TIME

HARLEQUIN ROMANCE

2659—TOUCH OF GOLD

These books may be available at your local bookseller.

Don't miss any of our special offers. Write to us at the following address for information on our newest releases.

Harlequin Reader Service
901 Fuhrmann Blvd., P.O. Box 1397, Buffalo, NY 14240
Canadian address: P.O. Box 603,
Fort Erie, Ont. L2A 9Z9

To Touch the Stars
Pamela Browning

Harlequin Books

TORONTO • NEW YORK • LONDON
AMSTERDAM • PARIS • SYDNEY • HAMBURG
STOCKHOLM • ATHENS • TOKYO • MILAN

This book is dedicated to the memory
of my two wonderful grandmothers,
and also to Caroline Zabonik Browning,
who makes delicious goulash.

Published October 1986

First printing August 1986

ISBN 0-373-16170-0

Copyright © 1986 by Pamela Browning. All rights reserved.
Philippine copyright 1986. Australian copyright 1986.
Except for use in any review, the reproduction or utilization of
this work in whole or in part in any form by any electronic,
mechanical or other means, now known or hereafter invented,
including xerography, photocopying and recording, or in any
information storage or retrieval system, is forbidden without
the permission of the publisher, Harlequin Enterprises Limited,
225 Duncan Mill Road, Don Mills, Ontario, Canada M3B 3K9.

All the characters in this book have no existence outside the
imagination of the author and have no relation whatsoever to
anyone bearing the same name or names. They are not even
distantly inspired by any individual known or unknown to the
author, and all incidents are pure invention.

The Harlequin trademarks, consisting of the words
HARLEQUIN AMERICAN ROMANCE, HARLEQUIN
AMERICAN ROMANCES, and the portrayal of a Harlequin,
are trademarks of Harlequin Enterprises Limited; the portrayal
of a Harlequin is registered in the United States Patent and
Trademark Office and in the Canada Trade Marks Office.

Printed in Canada

THE ANDRASSY FAMILY

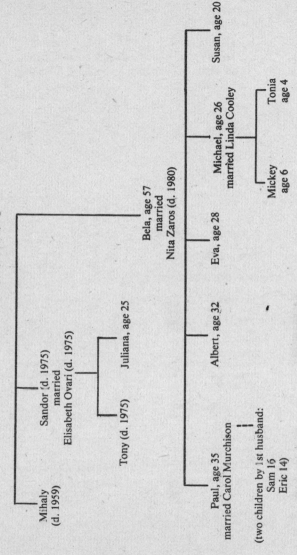

Anton Andrassy (d. 1975)
married
Marta Kanyo (Nonna) age 76

Mihaly
(d. 1959)

Sandor (d. 1975)
married
Elisabeth Ovari (d. 1975)

Tony (d. 1975)   Juliana, age 25

Bela, age 57
married
Nita Zaros (d. 1980)

Paul, age 35
married Carol Murchison

(two children by 1st husband:
Sam 16
Eric 14)

Albert, age 32

Eva, age 28

Michael, age 26
married Linda Cooley

Mickey
age 6

Tonia
age 4

Susan, age 20

*"Some say that only a fool walks the high wire.
But am I a fool to want to touch the stars?"*
—Stephen Andrassy

Prologue

January 1983

From the Associated Press:

MOSCOW CIRCUS STAR DEFECTS
IN LAST-MINUTE ESCAPE

MIAMI —In a daring run for freedom, Moscow Circus headliner Stephen Andrassy defected to the United States Wednesday.

Andrassy was at the airport in Havana, Cuba, preparing to board a Soviet Aeroflot jet with fellow members of the Moscow Circus troupe. Instead of filing aboard the Soviet plane as scheduled, Andrassy dashed one hundred yards to a Worldwide Airlines 727 that was preparing to taxi down the runway prior to takeoff.

A Worldwide flight attendant reported that Andrassy yelled, "I'm going with you! Tell the pilot to take off!"

The Worldwide plane, which had been hijacked from Miami to Cuba by a lone gunman on Tuesday, left Havana with Andrassy on board. Authorities say that the hijacking was not related to Andrassy's defection.

Andrassy is one of the top stars of the world-renowned Moscow Circus, where he performs a daring high-wire act.

"I am seeking asylum, and I hope to become a citizen of the United States as soon as possible," said Andrassy when he disembarked at the Miami airport late Wednesday night, where he was greeted by United States immigration officials.

Chapter One

Julie Andrassy held her breath. Dusty shafts of light streaked through the high window overhead, illuminating the gymnast on the balance beam. A swing roll, a V split, a walkover. Then Julie's best student tipped her body into a move called the needle scale. One leg supported her and one angled up in the air; then the gymnast nimbly bent her torso downward so that her head touched her supporting leg.

Julie exhaled slowly. She needn't have worried. Molly, at age twelve, was good, very good. Her routine was almost flawless.

"That was wonderful, Molly," Julie called as Molly dismounted with a leap. "Your routine looks super. Be careful to keep your supporting leg straight, though."

Molly wiped her face with a towel. "I'm having trouble with that move today," she said.

"Maybe it's because you're not fully recovering from your stag leap before you go into the needle scale. Here, I'll show you."

Julie mounted the beam with a front split, swinging her supple body into Molly's routine easily and naturally. The light from the window washed her olive skin with a golden tint, and her long ponytail danced behind her. Molly watched intently from the corner of the gym, and the man who had come searching for Julie watched, too.

The routine lasted one minute and ten seconds, a minute and ten seconds in which the moves required Julie's utter concentration. It wasn't until she was in midair with her dismounting leap that she saw the fair-haired man standing in the doorway of the gym.

"That was *perfect*," Molly told her. She tossed the towel in Julie's direction. "I'll try it again." Molly leaped onto the balance beam and began her routine with a body wave.

Julie bit her lip, mentally going through the balance beam exercises with Molly, move by move.

"She is a very good student," the man said as Molly dismounted. He had stepped out of the shadows of the doorway and stood directly behind Julie.

Julie swiveled her head around. She didn't know this man, and she knew he didn't belong in the gym of the Venice Gymnastics Club. It was after hours, and he didn't work there; neither was he the father of one of her students. She opened her mouth to ask him to leave, and that was when she got her first look into his eyes.

They were dark blue, darkest blue, and they were set deep beneath a prominent ridge of bone. That face, that face with its strong, square jaw, its high Slavic cheekbones—Julie had seen that face before. She had seen it many times before in Nonna's precious pictures.

"Stephen?" she said incredulously. "Is it you?"

"It is," he said.

She had known he would be here one day, but she hadn't been prepared for him to arrive so soon.

"I've been expecting you," she said slowly, and she held out her hand.

"I HAVE HAD AN OFFER from the Big Apple Circus. There I would be a star. But this is not what I want. What I want is for the Amazing Andrassys to walk the wire again together." This conversation was taking place a half hour later over a cup of coffee at the café down the street.

"It won't work, Stephen. Take the job." Julie knew of the Big Apple Circus; it was a one-ring stationary circus located in New York City. Circus people who didn't like traveling preferred to work for this particular show because it provided an opportunity to settle in one place.

"Juliana, I need you," Stephen said earnestly. "The Amazing Andrassys need you."

Julie leaned her chin on her hand and stared down at the scrunched-up paper wrapper from the straw in her Coke. She dipped a fingertip in her glass of water and dribbled a few drops on the wrinkles in the wrapper. Slowly the wrinkles unbuckled; the wrapper twisted and turned. She looked up to find Stephen staring at her with a puzzled expression.

"What is this?" he said, gesturing at the now-sodden paper wrapper. "What is this? Old American custom?"

Julie grinned. "Nonna always did that to keep me amused in restaurants when I was small. We ate in restaurants a lot, traveling with the act."

"So—is not old American custom. It is a *Nonna* custom, no?" He smiled.

Julie shrugged. Then she sighed. It was painful to talk about it, but she knew she must. "It won't work, Stephen. Putting the act back together, I mean."

"What? In America everything is possible. I believe this. Why don't you?" His blue eyes stabbed into her.

"You don't understand. You don't know what it did to us when the Amazing Andrassys fell." *What it did to me,* she thought, but she didn't say the words.

"Ah," he said. He was silent for a while.

"The others—Michael, Albert, Paul, Béla. And Eva. How do they feel?"

"Uncle Béla's injury was too severe for him ever to go back on the high wire. He clerks in a store in Kentucky."

"The others?"

"Michael has a good job as a catcher with the Flying Cordonis at a circus-theme amusement park in Texas. I can't see him giving it up."

"Albert? Paul?"

"Albert is working with a small truck-show circus in Mexico. We don't even know where to find him. Paul has given up the circus. He married a woman with two children and lives on a farm in Georgia. He is happy, Stephen. I don't think you can depend on Paul. And Eva—she has recently gone through a painful divorce. She's working as an aerobics instructor in Sarasota. And she hates the high wire."

"But you, Juliana. You have so much talent. I watched you on the balance beam. Such grace! You want to see the Amazing Andrassys back on the high wire again, do you not?"

"I have a good job as a gymnastics coach. One of my students may be Olympic material. I like my job, and I never want to go on the high wire again. Never!" Her eyes, black as night, flashed fiery sparks.

"I cannot believe you mean this," he said slowly, refusing to give up on her.

"But I do," she said.

"Have you not felt the lightness, the peace of giving yourself up to the wire completely? The centering down in yourself, that moment of concentration when you are one with the air? Haven't you?" The ferocity in his expression frightened her.

"I have felt it," she whispered, "but I can't anymore."

"You will again if you want to! I know it!"

There was something desperate behind those expressive bright blue eyes, something almost hypnotizing about their intensity. But Julie could never forget the horrors of that night in New Orleans, not even for this man who had traveled so far, who had taken such a chance.

Julie wadded the paper wrapper and tossed it into an ashtray. She looped the handle of her duffel bag over her arm and stood up.

"Stephen, the Amazing Andrassys no longer exist," she said fiercely. "Leave us alone. Leave us *alone*."

She whirled and ran out of the restaurant so that she wouldn't have to see the expression in his eyes.

"AND THIS—this is your mother, Stephen. You look like her." Nonna's gnarled finger trembled as she pointed at a faded photograph carefully pasted in a red leather album. Other photos, some brown with age, were scattered across the butcher-block Formica top of the kitchen table.

Julie leaned closer to inspect the photo of Stephen's mother. Yes, Stephen did look like his mother, the lovely Tina Martinovic of the Martinovic Magicians.

"Tina was like my own daughter," Nonna said. "Our families went back a long way together in the Hungarian circus tradition. I loved her. And you, my Stephen. I cared for you when you were a tiny towheaded boy. How I have hoped that I would see you one more time before I die. And now you are here. My prayers have been answered."

"Nonna," Stephen said gently. "All your wishes should come true. I would make them true for you if I could. And your big wish—to see the Amazing Andrassys on the high wire again—I want to make this wish come true above all others."

Nonna's faded gray eyes blinked up at him from a brown face mazed with wrinkles. "This cannot be," she said, her voice quavering. "My sons Mihaly and Sandor are dead. My son Béla is so crippled that he will never walk the wire again. My grandchildren do not care. Our art, our livelihood are no more."

Stephen knelt beside her chair. "Nonna, *I* care. I want to put the act together again."

"You, Stephen? You would do this?"

"I will make the others care. I will do this out of my pride in the Andrassy name. And for you, Nonna."

"My husband, Julie's Grandfather Anton, would not have liked to see the wonderful tradition of the Andrassys end. He would be so unhappy if he knew that the Andrassys had given up the wire. The wire! It lived for him, the wire. It sang, he said, it talked to him. It was his livelihood and his life. He loved the high wire, and he taught his family to love it, too. But then, after the accident, the heart of the Andrassys was stilled."

"I want to be the heart of the Andrassys," said Stephen. "I want to be the one to bring the Andrassys together again."

"If only you could. If only..." Nonna's words trailed off and she stared into space as though reliving other times, seeing other places.

"Stephen," Julie began. She would not have him upsetting Nonna, who at seventy-six was frail and failing.

"Let her hear me, Juliana." He turned again to Nonna. "I want to find Michael and Paul and Albert. I want to talk to Eva. I want to convince Juliana that the Amazing Andrassys must walk the wire again. Together."

This was too much for Julie. "Nonna, Stephen has had an offer from the Big Apple Circus in New York City. They've offered him star billing and a fantastic salary as a solo performer. We don't need the Amazing Andrassys anymore." She shot a meaningful glance at Stephen and got up from her chair, stalking to the sink, where she ran the water noisily and pretended to wash a few glasses.

"This is true?" whispered Nonna, looking uncertainly at Stephen.

"Yes," Stephen acknowledged. "But it is not for this—a magnificent salary, star billing—that I came to America. I came because I wanted to get our family back together again."

"This is my wish, too," Nonna said wonderingly. "This is my dream. My Anton would have wanted it."

Julie turned off the water. She could stand no more of this conversation. "Stephen, you forget. You're not an Andrassy."

Stephen stood and regarded her with an expression of incredulity. "I am not an Andrassy? I want to be the heart of the Andrassys. And in my soul I *am* an Andrassy."

"You were born a Martinovic. I thought your name was Martinovic-Andrassy." Julie crossed her arms implacably over her chest.

"Yes, I was born a Martinovic. But Nonna cared for me from the time I was a baby, and I was to go on the high wire with the Andrassys. The great Anton Andrassy said so himself, did he not, Nonna?"

"Yes, my husband said you had the soul for it. The soul of an Andrassy."

"And that is why I took the Andrassy name. It is the only name I have ever used as a performer. 'What is your name?' they asked me when I was six years old and I was sent to the Soviet school for circus performers. I was proud to say 'Andrassy,' a great name in the Hungarian circus for five generations."

"You have earned the right to the Andrassy name," Nonna said as though she would brook no argument.

Julie turned away, sickened. More talk like this would cause nothing but trouble. "I'm going for a walk," she said, disgustedly throwing the dish sponge into the bottom of the sink, where it landed with a loud splat. And then, for the second time that day, she fled from Stephen Andrassy.

THE RUBBER HEELS of her gym shoes made no sound on the sidewalk as Julie marched down the street of the subdivision in Venice, Florida, where she and

Nonna lived in a small three-bedroom concrete-block bungalow. Impatiently she flipped a long wavy lock of hair back from her face; she wished she hadn't loosened it from its rubber band. She dug her hands deep into the pockets of the warm-up suit she still wore over her practice leotard, but she found nothing there with which to bind her hair, not even a loose thread. She unzipped her jacket. The night was warm for January.

Was she wrong? Should she support Stephen in his push to get the Andrassys back on the high wire?

No. She must harden her heart against his insane idea. The past was the past.

The Andrassys had broken with the past often enough before, for instance, when they had left Hungary during the 1956 revolution, penniless refugees fleeing a Soviet invasion. That was when their family, the real Andrassys, had been separated from Tina Martinovic, who, since the death of her husband and the dissolving of their act, had worked as wardrobe mistress for the Andrassys. Left behind with Tina was her son Stephen. Tina's death in the aftermath of the invasion had made Stephen an orphan.

Bureaucratic red tape had made it impossible to effect a reunion with the boy. Stephen and the Andrassys' fame as circus stars were abandoned in Hungary. When authorities learned that he was an orphan, Stephen had been chosen to attend the select Moscow Circus school. The Andrassys had traveled to America, and they had never looked back.

The Amazing Andrassys had put together their high-wire act on this side of the Atlantic. They had learned to love the United States. Their act was well known and respected. They settled in Venice, Flor-

ida, winter home of the Ringling Bros. and Barnum &
Bailey Circus, with whom they performed for several
years. As soon as possible, they all became naturalized citizens. Julie and her cousins Michael and Susan had all been born in the United States.

Finally, there had been that tragic night eight years
ago at the Louisiana Superdome in New Orleans. The
fall. In the plunge from the cable high above the
arena, Grandfather Anton was killed. Julie's mother
and father and brother were killed. Uncle Béla was
seriously injured. Eva and Albert and Michael had
been injured, too, although not seriously.

On that fateful night, Julie had not gone on the high
wire with the others. She had remained on the ground,
and thus she had watched in horror as the famous
Andrassy pyramid fell apart in midair. She had not
been hurt—at least not physically. Nevertheless, her
wounds were deep, deeper than anyone knew, for she
alone knew the terrible sequence of events that day.

Without Grandfather Anton, there was no one with
the expertise to pull the act together again. The new
generation of Andrassys had no heart for the high wire
after the fall that had taken so many of their loved
ones.

Deep in thought, reliving the sadness yet one more
time, Julie didn't hear Stephen's light steps approaching from behind.

"Juliana," he said.

She moved over on the sidewalk, making room for
him to walk beside her. A sideways glance told her that
he had not given up his crazy idea. His eyes pierced
through her from beneath brows drawn together in
determination, and his chin was firmly set. A lock of

wheat-colored hair whipped across his forehead in the steady breeze from the Gulf of Mexico close by.

"You might as well call me Julie," she said. "Everyone else does."

He regarded her for a long moment, taking in her wispy dark hair flying behind her as she walked, the big dark eyes fringed with long black lashes. Two dusky spots of color heightened the glow of her light olive complexion.

"No," he said shortly. "I shall call you Juliana."

She shrugged. It made no difference what he called her. He would be leaving soon, she supposed. He'd soon come to understand that steady work and top billing with the Big Apple Circus were not to be sneezed at. Maybe she could convince him.

"You should take that job with the circus," she told him. "It's a good offer, one that any performer would be proud to get. It's not too late to say yes—you could still join them."

"Oh? Am I not welcome in Nonna's home?"

"It's not that, Stephen. I'm glad, and I'm sure all the Andrassys are glad, that you are in the United States. We want you here. But we don't want to be part of your act."

"I will stay with you, then, for a while. Until I decide what to do. I am going to become a citizen of your country, you know. I have established residency, and it will be five years before I can take my citizenship oath."

Julie said nothing. Stephen easily kept up with her, swinging along with a springy step and the ease of an athlete. Julie stole a look at his lean-muscled arms. No flab there or anywhere else. Stephen would be—let's see, he'd be thirty-five. He was ten years older than she was. And he had been walking the high wire almost all of his life. It was a calling that demanded the most of a performer, physically as well as mentally. No wonder he was in such good shape.

Stephen said, "I have much to learn about your country. Your language—"

"You speak excellent English," she said. He spoke with a decidedly British accent.

"I practiced. Always I knew that I would become a citizen of the United States of America. Always I knew that I would someday be back with Nonna and my family. I learned English in Hungary as a child. Then, in the Soviet Union I insisted that a fellow performer who knows the language well speak to me only in English. I was clever, don't you think?" He lifted his eyebrows and looked earnestly down at her. He wanted her approval.

"Yes, very clever," she said reluctantly.

"And with the act I will be clever, too. With enough Andrassys we can do the pyramid again."

"The pyramid! But that's what the Andrassys were doing when—" Julie stared at him. She was stricken speechless.

"I know. But the pyramid was so beautiful. A superb show of skill, concentration and teamwork. The Andrassy pyramid—yes, we will do it once more." He fairly vibrated with enthusiasm.

But his self-assurance was too much for Julie. Her eyes flashed angrily. "You may want to be the heart of the Andrassys. You may want to be the soul of the Andrassys. But I—*I* am their conscience!"

"Juliana—"

"No!" The word burst from her and she began to sprint back toward the safe haven of Nonna's house.

She ran past low concrete-block houses painted in rainbow colors and surrounded by banks of croton and hibiscus. She ran past a streetlight and on into the dark beyond, and then into the circle of light from the next streetlight.

Stephen caught up with her. He tried to grab her wrist, but she wrenched it away. She ran on, running easily and lightly. As an athlete in the peak of condition, she could run forever if she had to.

There was a little park at the end of the cul-de-sac. It was a playground with a few swings and monkey bars for the kids, and there were wide-slatted benches where the retired people who lived nearby liked to sit in the sun and watch the children. When she realized that Stephen had more than enough stamina to run as long as she did, Julie stopped running and sank down onto one of the benches under a streetlight. The swings cast eerie shadows on the cypress basket-weave fence that separated the park from the houses next to it.

She was trembling, and she wrapped her arms around her to ward off her sudden chill. How could she have thought she could outrun either Stephen or his ideas? Stephen was in even better shape than she was, and he had made it clear that her opposition wasn't enough to make him give up his hopes that the Andrassys would once again walk the wire together.

"Juliana, I am sorry if I made you think of something unpleasant. I don't wish to make you unhappy. I only want you to listen to what I want to do. To listen to Nonna. She wants the Andrassys back on the high wire." Stephen sat down beside her. His expression was honest and sincere; she knew he thought that he was right.

"I won't have you upsetting my grandmother," she said coldly. "She isn't in the best of health. She has already had one heart attack, and I don't want her to have another."

"I don't wish to upset her. I would never hurt Nonna in any way. But I want her to have what she has always wanted and what I want too—the Amazing Andrassys, together again!"

"The other Andrassys are unavailable. I told you that."

"I have not talked with them. I don't know how they feel." There was a stubborn glint to his eyes. She stared at him, wondering at this man. He had arrived in the United States only a few weeks ago. He barely knew any of them, except through Nonna's faithful letters over the years. What made him think he could change anyone's mind?

"Stephen," she began, groping for words. What more could she say? Hadn't she made her stand perfectly clear?

"There are many things I need to learn about your country. I will need help, Juliana. Yours and Nonna's. I need to know how to make change from a one-dollar bill. I need to know how the microwave oven works. I have to find out how to make a long-distance phone call. I need correction for my pronunciation of your language. Will you help me?"

He was so close that she could hardly breathe. He was so close that she smelled the clean, fragrant scent of him, a scent unlike that of any cologne-sprayed American man she knew. Stephen smelled like something fresh and green, like—yes, that was it—like new-mown hay she had seen from a car window on one trip across Kansas when she was a little girl and they traveled by car to all the major cities in the Midwest, following the circus with which they'd been performing. She had rolled down the window and let the hay scent blow into her hair, into her mouth.

And he was not of her blood, not of Andrassy blood. Her heart speeded up with the realization that she found him attractive in a way that was not familial at all. A strangling tightness cramped her heart, and she turned her eyes away, unable to look into his eyes any longer.

He touched a strand of her fine dark hair and lifted his other hand to press against her cheek, turning her face slowly toward him.

"I didn't think you liked me," he said softly. "And now I know that you do. Thank you for that, Juliana. We can be friends, can we not?"

Friends. It was not too much to ask. She owed him that because Nonna loved him. Still uncertain of what he would do now, she nodded, and he took his hand away from her face. Her skin burned where he had touched it.

His voice was gentle, and he didn't smile. "I think we should go back to Nonna," he said. "I don't like leaving her all alone."

He stood; she stood. He waited for her to lead the way out of the park on the narrow path, past the swaying swings, past the children's slide. He didn't touch her again, and they walked in silence, each absorbed in private thoughts, all the way back to Nonna's.

Chapter Two

"Now here is a new phone number I haven't tried yet," Nonna said with satisfaction. She read from an ad in a magazine, peering down at it through her bifocals. " 'New campground franchise. Telephone the campgrounds for reservations.' " The glint in her eye was more than satisfaction. It was something approaching excitement.

"What is this?" Stephen asked, hovering over her. "I don't understand the American telephone system."

Julie walked in from work at that moment, carrying a full bag of groceries.

"Neither does anyone else, Stephen," she said. "So don't feel bad."

"Am I missing something?" Stephen asked the air. Julie had brushed past him into the kitchen, where she set about noisily opening and closing cupboard doors.

"Do you know what happened today, Julie?" Nonna called, striving to be heard over the clatter.

"Probably not," Julie retorted. She peeked around the kitchen door with a grin.

"What happened," Nonna said, "is that I phoned a number that had been changed from an airline reservations number to some place calling itself Sam's Resorts. What kind of place calls itself Sam's Resorts? A nice young man answers, but he never told me what is Sam's Resorts. A bookie, I think it is.''

"What is this all about?" Stephen asked. "What is this calling people? What is a bookie?"

"Nonna calls toll-free 800 numbers for a hobby," Julie explained. She decided not to explain what a bookie was unless pressed for further details.

"What is an 800 number?"

"It's a long-distance telephone number you can call with no charge. Companies have them. Nonna likes to call the airlines and make reservations." Julie shrugged and went back into the kitchen.

"I get lonely sitting here all day. Calling these numbers gives me a nice polite young person to talk to. There's always somebody at the airlines. I have called insurance companies, too, but they're not so much fun. Campgrounds and motels are not bad. But the airlines are the best. When they put me on hold, they play music." Nonna smiled up at Stephen complacently.

"You do this every day?"

"Some days. If it's an airline, I have to call back later and cancel the reservation. That's nice, too."

Julie peered around the kitchen door to see that Stephen still wore a look of puzzlement. She had an idea that he found life in America confusing so far. He certainly asked a lot of questions. What is a massage parlor? he'd wanted to know. How do those old ladies make their hair blue? Where do they grow those singers on MTV?

Now Stephen stared at the phone. "I guess, then, you are the person, Nonna, to tell me how to make long-distance phone calls."

"It is very simple. You just—"

"Long-distance phone calls?" Julie reappeared from the kitchen as though summoned like a genie from a bottle.

"To call the Andrassys. First I will call Paul. Then I will call Michael. Then I will—"

"Stephen, I *told* you—"

"You told me. That is enough. Now it is up to me to find out for myself what the Andrassys think."

"You're wasting your time," Julie said darkly. She tossed a bibbed apron over her head and tied it in back.

"Julie, Stephen only wants the Amazing Andrassys back on the high wire. This is good, I think." Nonna pinched her lips together and fixed Julie with a glare of her own. When Nonna got her dander up, there was no bucking her authority. Julie preferred things not to get to that point. In deference to Nonna's health, she usually backed down first.

"Okay," she said, turning her back on them. "Okay." She went back in the kitchen and fretted impotently as she heard Stephen say, "Oh, so I must dial the number one first and then the area code? And then the other numbers?"

Let him call the others and present his ridiculous idea, fumed Julie inwardly. That was the best way for Stephen to find out what he was up against. She knew that none of the other Andrassys would be interested in a new act.

After dinner, while Julie cleaned up the kitchen with Nonna's help, Stephen went into the living room and sat down on the couch. He carefully dialed one of the numbers Nonna had shown him in her small flowered address book, and she heard him talking quietly. She tried to ignore the hushed tones of Stephen's conversation, and when Stephen called Nonna to the phone, she turned on the garbage disposal so she couldn't hear Nonna speak.

But she couldn't run the garbage disposal forever.

"Juliana!"

She turned to find Stephen standing behind her with the flowered address book in his hand, and he was smiling broadly.

"Michael is interested. He wants me to call the others."

Julie felt all the air leave her lungs in one surprising rush. "Michael? I don't believe it."

"It is true, isn't it, Nonna?"

Nonna beamed up at him. "It *is* true, Julie. Michael does not like his job. There is not enough excitement, he says, in being a catcher for the Flying Cordonis."

"But Michael always said he'd never walk the high wire again." Julie was dismayed at her cousin's change of mind.

"It has been a long time," Nonna said gently. "A long time since that night of the fall in New Orleans. And Michael has two children. He has to think of their future as Andrassys."

"Their *future*! Why would he want their future to be working a high-wire act?" Julie spit the words out bitterly.

Nonna's expression became stern. "Because of his loyalty to family tradition, Julie! That is something you need more of, perhaps!" Nonna bit down on her lips and stumped out of the room, leaving Julie blinking at Stephen.

"Do not be angry," Stephen said. At the moment, his eyes were filled with compassion for her.

Julie lifted her hands and let them fall helplessly.

"Now I will call Uncle Béla," Stephen said. "Would you like to listen?"

"I—I'm going back to the gym for a late practice session with Molly," she said. "She has an important meet this weekend."

Stephen nodded and went back to the living room, where he picked up the phone receiver and began to dial a number. Julie grabbed her pocketbook and rushed out the door just as Stephen was saying, "Uncle Béla? This is Stephen. Yes, Stephen Andrassy."

She could not bear to stay and listen to him as he employed his considerable powers of persuasion. Neither could she stand any more of Nonna's scathing disapproval.

And she hated to be accused of anything less than total family loyalty. After all, it was her affection for the others that made her feel that subjecting themselves to the danger of the high wire again would be a terrible mistake—a terrible, terrible mistake.

IT WAS AFTER ELEVEN O'CLOCK when Julie crept into the house after a long workout with Molly at the gym. She closed the front door quietly behind her and tiptoed down the hall. The guest bedroom where Stephen slept showed a thin line of light beneath the door, indicating that he was still awake.

Julie hurried to the bathroom and peeled off her leotard, running the shower until it was very hot. She showered quickly, letting the hot water sluice over her tight muscles. She had put in a total of ten working hours today; the hours had taken their toll along with the emotional tug-of-war with Stephen, and she felt exhausted.

She slipped into her nightgown and long velour robe and padded across the hall to her room, where she shut the door and turned down the bed. She was about to slide between the sheets when she heard Stephen's hesitant tap on her door.

"Juliana?" His tongue wrapped around the syllables of her name with only the hint of an accent. No one else had ever spoken her name quite that way. No one else, of course, ever called her Juliana.

"Just a minute," she called out, re-wrapping her robe around her.

Stephen stood in the doorway, looking apologetic. He wore the clothes he had worn earlier—a pair of navy blue pants, a sport shirt open at the neck and a new pair of Docksiders, with no socks.

"I wanted to speak with you about the others," he said. His blue eyes were solemn.

"Well, don't stand out there. You'll wake Nonna. Come in." Julie held the door wide and stood aside so that he could enter her room. He looked around uncomfortably. She waved a hand at the yellow vinyl beanbag chair in the corner. "Make yourself comfortable," she told him.

He lifted his pale eyebrows into twin peaks, but then he gamely folded himself into the chair, appearing momentarily disconcerted at the pop of the Styrofoam pellets inside the vinyl cover. Julie suppressed a smile. She was sure that Stephen had never encountered a beanbag chair before. She wondered what he thought of it, then wisely decided not to ask.

"I have talked with Uncle Béla. As you told me, he cannot work the high wire again because of his injury. But he wished me luck. And he said that his daughter has been asking if the Andrassys will ever have an act again."

Julie sank down on the edge of the bed. "Susan?"

"Yes, Susan. I spoke to her on the telephone tonight and she is very interested. She was not with you in New Orleans?"

"No, Susan was only twelve years old at that time. She was enrolled in school here in Venice."

Susan, little Susan, with her long, skinny brown pigtails, had always been a favorite of Julie's. After the fall, how glad Julie had been that Susan had not joined the act yet, at least officially. Susan, of course, had trained to go on the high wire from earliest childhood. But her parents had wanted her to have as normal a life as possible, and so Susan at twelve had not been in New Orleans. She had been home in Venice with Nonna.

"So," Stephen said with satisfaction. "I have recruited a new Andrassy."

"Susan said she would do it? Honestly?"

"She is teaching at a nursery school in Paducah, Kentucky. She is ready for a change."

Julie could say nothing. She wondered what promises Stephen had made, what lure he had held out in front of impressionable Susan.

"Juliana, I have also talked with Paul."

Julie shook her head. It was almost too much. Paul was the cousin who had married a Georgia widow with two boys of her own. Surely Paul, of all people, had not given any encouragement to Stephen's ridiculous idea?

"What did Paul say?"

"Paul does not want to perform in the act again. He is settled on his farm in Georgia and beginning a new career as a land developer. But he will support the rest of us."

"The rest of us? The rest of *you*, you mean!" Julie jumped up from her spot on the edge of the bed and strode to the dresser in the corner, fumbling in the Kleenex box for a tissue.

"Juliana, please don't cry! Please!" Seeming genuinely distressed, Stephen struggled his way out of the beanbag and came to stand behind her.

Julie buried her face in her hands. All she could see when she closed her eyes was a pile of bodies, spangled and bright in their matching blue leotards, a pile of bodies lying on the floor of the Superdome.

"Juliana! This must not bring you so much unhappiness! Can't you see that the odds are against such a terrible accident happening again?"

He rested his hands on her heaving shoulders, and she was barely conscious of his touch. It was hard for her to accept even the slightest kindness from Stephen when she perceived him as the catalyst that had brought all the old pain and grief out of the far region of her mind where she had hidden those emotions for the last eight years.

"Juliana?" he said, turning her around.

"Why don't you go away?" she whispered. "Nonna and I were very happy before you came."

For a moment his face lost its assurance, and the expression in his eyes seemed immeasurably sad.

"Dear Juliana," he said. "Do you think I have not thought of this? But there is the Hungarian circus tradition to think of also. The Andrassys—and the Martinovices, because I know you do not think of me as an Andrassy—we are circus families. Can we allow the tradition to die while we, great performing artists, take jobs as clerks and gymnastics instructors and teachers? Would Anton Andrassy approve? I know he would not."

She could not speak. Stephen was right. If Grandfather Anton had lived, he would have spearheaded a drive to get all the Andrassys back on the high wire immediately after the accident. He would have been ashamed of them for lacking courage.

"You see?" Stephen said, his eyes plumbing the murky depths of hers. "You see?"

"I'm afraid," she whispered. "I'm afraid."

His arms went around her, strong as steel bands. His body pressed against hers, and there was nothing weak or soft about him. He was solid, real. Yet she knew the gentleness of his eyes, his manner, his voice that even now spoke to her in low hushed tones.

"Don't be afraid, Juliana. You must trust me. Trust me as you trusted your family on the high wire. That trust is the most important thing of all. Trust me."

For a moment, lulled by his voice, betrayed by his words, Julie almost succumbed. Then she remembered what had really happened that night. She remembered the secret she had never told anyone.

She stiffened within the circle of his embrace and twisted away from him.

"Get out of my room! Get out!" She stood like a cornered animal, a wounded animal, hissing at him so that she would not wake Nonna.

"Juliana—"

"Out!"

Without a word he wheeled around and left. Julie flew to shut the door, then locked it. As she heard the click of his own door latch, she leaned against the door and closed her eyes, wishing she had never set them on Stephen Andrassy.

"I THOUGHT I'D NEVER get here! The traffic is so terrible out there—I don't think I've ever seen so many Northerners here for the winter season, have you?"

Julie rose from the booth and exchanged kisses with her cousin Eva. Eva was smartly dressed in a new white suit, which contrasted with her tanned olive complexion. Julie and Eva, who was three years older than Julie, resembled each other, except that Eva's black hair was not long and wavy like Julie's but straight and worn in a chic Dutch-boy bob.

"Now tell me about Stephen," Eva said when they had ordered lunch. "Don't leave anything out. Is he as handsome as his pictures?"

Julie thought about this. Her feelings on the subject of Stephen Andrassy were so conflicting that she had scarcely had time to think about him personally. At least not since that night in her bedroom.

"He's handsomer than his picture, I suppose. And he speaks English beautifully."

"That I know, Julie. I've talked with him on the phone, remember?"

"Yes," Julie said, her voice tinged with irony. "And talked with him and talked with him. What persuasive arguments does he use with you?"

Eva waved her hand. "Family loyalty. And Nonna. He's very big on throwing Nonna's name around. Tell

me, is Nonna that keen on seeing the Amazing Andrassys walk the high wire again? Or is this something Stephen has made up?''

Julie's shoulders slumped. ''I've never seen Nonna
like this, Eva. It's like he's fired her up on the subject
of the act. The act, the act, the act! It's all Nonna talks
about anymore. That and Grandfather Anton. That
he would have wanted the Andrassys together on the
high wire again.''

''I suppose he would have.'' Eva tossed her short
hair back and fixed Julie with a serious stare. ''And
how about you, Julie? How do you feel now?''

''I haven't changed my mind. I won't do it.''

''Mmm. That's what I figured.'' Eva's gaze faltered and fell to the tabletop. Then she raised her eyes
to Julie's. ''I might as well tell you, Julie. I'm seriously thinking about it.''

Julie stared, dumbfounded. ''You're what?''

Eva nodded. ''Yes,'' she said quietly.

''How can you, Eva? How can you even consider it?
Don't you remember standing in the corridor of
Charity Hospital in New Orleans after they'd taped up
your arm? You got hysterical when we couldn't find
out how Grandfather Anton was, and I had to slap
your face to calm you down. And after they came out
and told us about the others, you swore you'd never
go near a cable again, that you'd never—''

''Julie,'' Eva said patiently, ''that was eight years
ago. I was twenty years old. Since then I've weath-
ered a bad marriage and a devastating divorce. I've
given up on the idea of ever having children. I like
teaching aerobics, sure, but I can't see myself doing it
for the rest of my life. I need something more, some-

thing to strive for. Something all-encompassing. Working to get the act back together would be that."

Julie shook her head. She felt faint. "Eva," she whispered.

Eva's chin shot up. "I'm going to tell Stephen I'll do it. I'm going to go to see him today, at Nonna's."

"Eva," Julie whispered again. She could not believe it. Her cousin had been even more adamant about never going up on the high wire than she, Julie, had been.

"Please, Julie, do try to understand. I *need* this. I need something to give my life meaning again."

Julie could only continue to shake her head in disbelief. Never, in all her wildest imaginings, could she have thought that Eva, too, would sell out.

"I HOPE YOU DON'T MIND," Stephen said apologetically as Julie steered her car through lunch-hour traffic on the following Monday.

"Of course not," she said.

"If I didn't really need a haircut—"

"It's all right, Stephen. I had to come home from work to check on Nonna, anyway. She's been forgetting her pills lately."

"After this, if I'm there, I'll see that she takes them," Stephen said. He paused for a moment. "You know, Juliana, you are a very good driver. Driving is something I never learned to do. One doesn't need to know how to drive in Moscow. But here, everyone drives."

"You'll have to learn."

"I will. To have to call a taxi cab just to go get a haircut, I must admit that I feel very—how would you say?—*frustrated* not to be able to go anywhere on my own.''

Julie parked the car in front of the unisex hairdresser shop.

''I'll come in with you,'' she said. ''Maybe I can convince Dora to trim my split ends.''

''Cut your hair?'' Stephen said, sounding alarmed. ''Oh, I am not sure that you should do that.'' He focused his eyes on her ponytail as though fearful that it would disappear.

She softened toward him. ''Not cut my hair, Stephen. To trim my split ends means just to cut a half inch or so off the ends of the hair. See how the ends split and look white and funny?'' She twisted a strand of hair away from her ponytail's bulk and held it toward him.

He touched her hair with a tentative finger. ''Oh. I understand. Split ends. Well, you see, I am learning every day.'' He grinned at her jauntily, amused at himself.

Dora, who washed and set Nonna's hair once a week and who trimmed Julie's long hair when necessary, greeted them pleasantly. She sat Stephen down in her chair and brushed his abundant silky blond hair back from his face while Julie watched.

''You have very fine hair,'' she commented. ''And you're wearing it rather long in the back. Shall I cut it the same way you're wearing it?''

''I think I would like it shorter everywhere. This way it looks too European for America,'' Stephen said.

Dora set about her work, turning Stephen around in the chair so that he faced Julie. Stephen leafed through a magazine as she cut, but Julie watched with interest as Dora worked.

Stephen had the most beautifully shaped head. A well-shaped head was so important in a man, and Stephen's was nicely proportioned, neither too large nor too small for his body. There were no bumps or bulges marring its roundness, and he had a strong jawline complemented by a prominent brow. As Dora snipped and shaped, Stephen's features assumed a new importance, now that they weren't overpowered by the length of his hair.

Catching Julie observing him, he glanced at her in a questioning manner, then cast his eyes down again as a small acknowledging smile played across his lips. Julie looked away, flustered. He had known she was admiring him.

"All right," Dora said, sweeping the cape away. "How do you like it?"

"It is fine, just fine," Stephen told her expansively.

"Julie, I have time to do you if you'd like," Dora said.

Silently Julie sat down in the operator's chair. It felt warm from the heat of Stephen's body.

Dora unfastened Julie's ponytail so that her thick black hair tumbled around her shoulders.

"Just trim the ends?" Dora asked, fluffing her hair experimentally.

Julie nodded. Now it was her turn to sit uncomfortably while Stephen scrutinized her.

Suddenly he said, "Juliana, your hair is very beautiful."

"Thank you," she replied stiffly, embarrassed at the attention.

"I'd like to see Julie wear her hair down more often," Dora commented conversationally.

"I can't," Julie said. "I couldn't teach gymnastics with my hair falling in my eyes."

"But when you're not at work," Dora said, "you could brush it out from a side part, like this," and she worked swiftly to demonstrate. "See?" She turned Julie slowly in the chair, giving her a hand mirror so she could inspect the back.

"It looks very pretty that way," Stephen said in approval.

"It's not practical," Julie said flatly, handing the mirror back. She looked like a stranger to herself with her hair flowing in a loose wave over her forehead, all but obscuring one eye.

"Still, you might want to wear it that way when you go out," Dora insisted, getting back to her haircutting.

When it was over, Julie automatically began to bundle her hair back into its rubber band as Dora swept up the fallen hair on the floor.

"Don't do that," Stephen interrupted, his eyes bright.

Julie fumbled with the rubber band. The way he was looking at her, with the light of appreciation in his blue eyes, made her feel as though she were someone completely different from the Julie Andrassy she had always been.

She continued her efforts with the rubber band until, under the nervous tension of her fingers, it snapped.

"I'll get you a new one," Dora said.

"No," Stephen said, and his tone stopped the hairdresser in midstep.

"Oh, all right," Julie said, covering her confusion with impatience. Her hair flounced around her shoulders as she marched to the cashier to pay her bill.

After they had emerged into the too-bright sunlight and were walking toward her car, Stephen said suddenly, "Let me treat you to lunch. It's the least I can do for the trouble you've taken."

"I don't have much time," Julie protested.

"But you have to eat," he replied in a reasoning tone. "Look, let's go across the street to that McDonald's." Stephen had only recently discovered McDonald's, and at the childlike look of anticipation on his face, Julie didn't have the heart to say no. Anyway, lunch there would be quick, and they could eat outside in the picnic area.

Julie ordered a Big Mac, and Stephen ordered a quarter pounder with cheese and three large packs of french fries.

"Are you going to be able to eat all those fries?" Julie asked skeptically when she was seated across the table from him. Children laughed in the nearby playground area; a warm wind blew on her face. Ronald McDonald beamed benevolently down at them from the window.

"Only if you help," Stephen said, pushing one pack of french fries across the table at her.

"I eat mine with catsup," she said, squeezing the catsup out of its little foil packet.

"Do you mind if I try that?" Stephen asked.

She shook her head, forgetting momentarily that she had no ponytail. A forelock fell across her face, and with her hands sticky with catsup all she could do was blow upward to move the hair out of her eyes.

Stephen, reaching across for one of the fries with catsup, said, "Let me," and he extended a forefinger and slowly, musingly, with a smile both sweet and tender, tucked her hair behind her ear. The brief contact stopped her heart for one electrifying moment, and she was startlingly aware of Stephen's lean, hard body sitting across from her, of the strong, knowing, sympathetic look to his deep blue eyes, of the corded lines of his throat above the placket of the knit shirt he wore.

Then it was as though nothing had happened. Stephen ate a french fry, declared that he liked them better without catsup and proceeded to consume the rest of his lunch.

Julie, shaken by her swift response to Stephen's gesture, which managed to be both innocent and provocative at the same time, took care that her hair did not slip forward again. Stephen's touching of her hair had awakened her to the fact that he saw her as an attractive woman. As for herself, she knew that after today she would never again be totally unaware of Stephen as a unique, stimulating and sexy man who was fully aware of his powers of masculinity.

Chapter Three

"Today," Nonna said as she and Julie were folding clean clothes together that evening, "I called a china company. They tried to sell me some bone china."

"You didn't buy any, I hope?" Julie said with some alarm. "The last thing we need is china." They were hard-pressed paying their bills as it was, even with her coaching job and Nonna's monthly Social Security check.

"No, I didn't buy any china, but some of the patterns sounded very lovely. They have one called 'Hungarian Rhapsody.' I was tempted to order it just to see what it looked like."

"Nonna, perhaps you should stop calling those toll-free 800 numbers. Have you ever thought that it might be illegal or something?" Julie scooped up a pile of Stephen's underwear with a frown. He wore stretchy little nylon briefs, all of them black.

"Don't you worry," Nonna replied with a sigh. "It is getting so that I can hardly use my own phone. Ring, ring, ring, that's all it does. Always it is for Stephen."

"And who calls him?" Julie asked, hating herself for asking. Still, she couldn't help being curious.

"That man from the Big Apple Circus called again today. He calls almost every day. And then Paul called—that was after Eva left the other day."

"Paul?"

"Yes, Paul. He and Stephen, they talk and talk."

"I don't need to wonder what it's about," Julie said, ducking across the hall to put the pile of underwear on Stephen's dresser. A slip of paper on the dresser caught her eye. It had long columns of figures written on it. In the brief moment in which she glanced at it, she couldn't make out what it was, and she had no business snooping in Stephen's things.

She rejoined Nonna in the living room. It was on the tip of her tongue to make a snide remark about what Stephen was doing, but by tacit agreement she and Nonna had avoided the topic of an Andrassy reunion on the high wire. Each knew how the other felt about the matter, and that was enough.

They had barely settled down to watch Nonna's favorite television program when the doorbell rang. Julie jumped up to answer it.

On the doorstep stood a familiar tall figure carrying a small valise. Julie threw the door open.

"Julie!" the man cried, enveloping her in a big hug.

"Albert, oh, Albert!" It was her cousin, the one no one had been able to locate, the one who had fled to Mexico after the accident to work with a truck-show circus.

Nonna hobbled to the door and she, too, was embraced.

"You must come in," Nonna said happily, marveling at the sudden appearance of her tall, bearded grandson. "It has been so long since I have seen you."

"Too long," Albert agreed, setting his battered valise down just inside the door and looking around as though he expected to see someone who wasn't there.

"You must tell us all your adventures," Nonna decreed. "Julie, please put on the coffeepot. And cut some of that caraway cake I made yesterday."

"I will," Julie said, favoring Albert with a big smile. She still could not believe he was here—Albert, her long-ago idol, brother of Paul and Eva and Michael and Susan! "But before I put the coffee on, I want to know what brings Albert home after seven long years."

Albert stared at her in perplexity. "Why, Julie, don't you know? I have come home to join Stephen. The circus grapevine brought me the news that he's starting up the act. I want to be part of the Amazing Andrassys!"

EARLY THE NEXT MORNING, the silence of the backyard was broken only by the warble of a cardinal flashing in and out of the palmetto leaves. Julie refilled the hummingbird feeder and stood back from it. If she waited long enough and quietly enough, some of her regulars might fly in for a bit of sugar syrup. And she had time; she wasn't due at the gym for another hour.

She heard the kitchen door swing open and slam shut, but she didn't turn her head. She knew who it was.

"They are all with me now, Julie," Stephen said, approaching from the direction of the house through grass damp with dew. "All of the Andrassys except you."

"And I will never be, Stephen. Never."

"Never say never," he said lightly. He went to the outdoor spigot and turned on the hose. He picked it up and refilled the concrete birdbath carefully. Julie watched him, taking in his newly acquired tan, the way dancing sunbeams glinted off his blond hair. Stephen finished filling the birdbath, turned the hose off and returned to stand beside her.

"I will miss this backyard of yours and Nonna's. It is very pretty here. You have done a lot with the plants and shrubs."

"Miss it? Are you going somewhere?" She turned to him; her heart, for some reason, seemed to stop in midbeat.

He studied her face carefully, as though committing it to memory. His eyes were clear and somehow serene, and they were the eyes of a man who was pleased with himself. She had never known anyone else who had the self-assurance of Stephen Andrassy. Or the stubbornness, either. Well, she could match him for stubbornness, she supposed. The thought made her lips twitch slightly in a near-smile.

"Oh, so you are glad I am leaving?" His voice was usually so gentle, even when she didn't like what he was saying, but now it was sharp.

What would their home be like without Stephen talking rapidly to her and Nonna in his funny Hungarian-British accent, without the phone ringing constantly for him, without his black underwear taking up room in the laundry basket? She had grown *used* to him. That was the word. She was *used* to him.

When she didn't answer, he said brusquely, "I am taking the Big Apple Circus offer."

The announcement was so abrupt and so unexpected that Julie said "Oh!" It was almost as if he'd slapped her. How could he go with the Big Apple show, now that he had the backing of everyone in the Andrassy family except her?

"I will go with the Big Apple Circus until the summer. They have offered a special contract that gives me three months of work at a very fine salary. And I will save my money. And when I return, I will have enough to pay for what we need to get the Amazing Andrassys back on the high wire."

She had not thought of the financial end of it. Yes, it would take money to do what Stephen wanted to do. Albert had quit his circus job in Mexico; Eva and Susan would have to quit their jobs, also. Michael had a wife and two children to support. Yet they would need to work full-time for months at getting the Amazing Andrassy act ready to play to an audience. Now she understood the columns of figures she'd seen on the paper on Stephen's dresser.

"That is very ambitious of you," she managed to say.

"It is good to be ambitious in America."

"When are you leaving?" she asked, looking at the red plastic flowers on the hummingbird feeder and not at him.

"Tomorrow. I will miss you, Juliana. And Nonna, of course."

"Of course," she murmured.

"I will return in three months. And when I return, I will want you to join the rest of us. You are an Andrassy above all else. You should not be clinging to the ground in fear. You, Juliana, should be touching the stars. Please think about it.'' His hand rested briefly on her arm.

"I already have, Stephen. And you know my answer." The words were faint.

"It will never be too late to change it," he said, squaring his shoulders. Then he strode away toward the house, leaving her quite alone.

A hummingbird swooped down out of the allamanda vine to feed, its wings flashing green fire. But Julie didn't take the pleasure in its presence that she normally did. All she could think about was that Stephen was leaving.

And that she would miss him, in spite of everything.

STEPHEN WAS LONELY in New York. Despite the standard of living that being a major star with the circus provided, he missed living at Nonna's house.

He was a man of solitude. All his life he had been lonely. Well, perhaps not all his life. The first six years of it were spent as an honorary Andrassy, and what Andrassy could be lonely with that wonderful sense of fellowship that prevailed when Andrassys were together?

He remembered Grandfather Anton, with his hair that was so white even in those days, and the way Grandfather Anton had held him in his lap and fascinated him with stories of the circus. Oh, Stephen had delighted in all the funny stories about clowns and animals and temperamental performers, about enthusiastic circus fans and about grumpy circus owners. All of the Andrassys had lived and breathed circus life in those days.

And Nonna. How gentle she had been when he had the measles, nursing him through his high fever and making her wonderful chicken broth just for him. How kind she had been to him and to his mother when his father had drowned in Budapest, victim of a freak boating accident on the Danube River. To Stephen, Nonna was the grandmother he had never known.

And now, once again, he had a chance to become part of the wonderful Andrassy family. The way Stephen saw it, he owed the Andrassys a debt of gratitude. They had taken care of him and his mother in the old days, and now he would repay them for their kindness. He was one of the few people in the world who had the expertise to help them put their fabulous high-wire act together again.

Could just anyone do this? No. Not everyone knew how to stretch a cable. Not everyone knew about the exact placing of the cavallettis. Not everyone knew about turnbuckles and hoist hooks and pulley blocks. And was all this important? Why, of course! A wire walker's life depended on his equipment.

They were with him now, all except for Juliana. Stephen despaired of this woman. Why didn't she trust him? The others did. What was it about Juliana that made her tremble when she thought about that night in New Orleans when the Andrassys had fallen from the wire? It was eight years ago, after all. The others had gotten over their trauma. Why hadn't Juliana?

If only she would talk to him. But she tightened up whenever he brought up the subject. What a waste it would be if Juliana continued to refuse to become a part of the new Amazing Andrassy act! She was a graceful, concentrated and controlled performer—he had seen that when he'd watched her demonstrate on the balance beam for her student.

It wasn't lack of skill that kept her from joining the act. Perhaps it was lack of nerve. Some people simply couldn't think well in stressful situations; when something went wrong, they fell apart. Such performers would do well to stay off a high wire—too much depended on the ability to stay calm, no matter what. He had no idea if this was Julie's problem.

Another reason for Julie to refuse to participate in the new act might be an aversion to him. Stephen refused to believe that this was it. He could make her laugh with his questions about life in America. She felt comfortable around him; he was sure of it. He wasn't positive that she liked him, though. Or maybe she liked him but wouldn't admit it.

He desperately tried to figure her out. It pained him that she was so obstinate about staying off the wire. Why wouldn't she see that he only wanted the family together again? And he *would* get the family together again, even if he had to bankroll such an operation himself.

That was the sole reason he had taken the circus job. The money was important. When he'd first sought asylum in the United States, he had not realized that a headliner with a major circus could earn so much money. It had taken several weeks in America to find out just what so much money could buy. But he didn't want a car. He didn't want a lot of clothes or a fancy house. What he wanted was what he had always wanted—to walk with the Andrassys on the high wire.

So he lived in Manhattan and he performed his exciting solo act high above the circus's one ring, and it was the highlight of the show. He rode a unicycle on the high wire and juggled as he rode. He performed somersaults on the wire. He did flips on the wire. He even cooked an omelet on the wire, and he ate it there, too. He walked the dangerous, blindfolded walk of death. As always, his strong presence as a performer impressed itself upon the audience, and he got wonderful reviews in all the papers.

He made friends in the circus. There were lots of women with the show, all kinds of women—women who rode horses bareback and women who flew through the air from trapeze to trapeze, women with silky blond hair so long they could sit on it, and women with breasts so prominent they reminded him of trays of fruit.

One of them took a special interest in him, and she filled what could have been lonely hours. Stephen was sure that she wanted their relationship to grow and deepen. Yet whenever he thought about letting that happen, he pulled back. He would not be with the circus longer than three months. And his thoughts were filled with visions of a pair of dark, snapping eyes and long curly hair wisped around a warm olive complexion. The woman to whom those characteristics belonged possessed a slim, fine-boned body with narrow hips and tiny breasts that barely swelled beneath her leotard. Beside her, all other women paled in comparison. Juliana. Even her name was beautiful.

Yet he had no reason to think that she found anything special in him, and this made him sad. What good was the admiration of the world when that one special person in it seemed determined to ignore him?

JULIE AND NONNA read about Stephen in the newspaper. A Soviet defector joining a New York City circus was news, especially in the close-knit community of circus stars and former circus stars in Venice, Florida.

"I saw that article about your cousin Stephen," said Julie's boss, who had once performed with a crack troupe of circus acrobats. "Sounds like he's doing well for himself."

"He's not my cousin," Julie said tensely before hurrying away to the dressing room.

"Say, that cousin of yours is really something," said the seven-foot-four-inch manager of the convenience store where Julie bought milk. The manager was a former circus clown himself.

"He's not my cousin," Julie said again.

Nonna cut out every newspaper article about Stephen and his daring exploits on the high wire. "He is a grandson to make me proud," Nonna said, snipping away.

"He is *not* your grandson," Julie protested faintly.

"Ach," Nonna said, inserting the clipping into her photo album. "That is something I forgot."

Everyone had accepted Stephen as a member of her family. Everyone, that is, except Julie herself.

She thought about him. She thought about him much too often. She thought about the curve of his eyelids, the flexibility of his fingers. She could picture his fingers tearing a piece of bread at dinner; she could picture them holding a fork in the tines-down European fashion. She, who was used to European ways, found Stephen's ways foreign and fascinating. He had not had time to become Americanized yet. He seemed exotic.

She thought about the timbre of his voice. It was a gentle voice with deep overtones and unusual inflections. It didn't twang or burr but glided smoothly over the English language like a brook over stones. His mouth was wide and well formed, with an upper lip that was a bit too long. It gave him a look that was decidedly sensual. Why had she noticed that?

Julie went on coaching in the gym, and she went on taking care of Nonna, making sure that Nonna took her blood-pressure medicine regularly, ate properly, didn't work too hard and got enough rest. She spoke with Eva on the telephone occasionally, and with Albert, who had traveled to Texas to visit Michael and his family. But they didn't talk about the act. Everyone knew how she felt about it; to touch the stars indeed! She didn't want to touch the stars; the ground was good enough for her.

Things almost settled down to normal, or at least to what Julie had recognized as normal before the arrival of Stephen.

Then, when she had forgotten about the curve of his eyelids and the flexibility of his fingers and the length of his upper lip, Stephen returned.

He was waiting for her outside the gym one afternoon in the first week in June.

"Stephen!" she exclaimed, her heart flipping over.

He pecked her cheek in a brotherly fashion. She pulled away. She still wore her leotard and she was sweaty from her workout on the beam. Her hair, smoothed back into a long ponytail, had escaped into damp little tendrils around her face.

"Aren't you glad to see me?" he asked with a merry twinkle in his eyes.

"Well..." She smiled back at him. He hadn't changed at all. He was still one of the best-looking men she'd ever seen.

"I took a cab over here just to meet you after work. I hope you have your car?"

"Yes, of course," she said, leading the way to the parking lot. A tiny frenetic poodle on a chain leaped toward them as it was being walked on the sidewalk; Stephen had to move closer to her to avoid stepping on the dog. For a moment she thought he was going to take her arm, but he didn't.

As they got into her car, Stephen said, "I've learned to drive. I have a license now."

"Oh?" Julie said. "How did you manage that?"

"One of the women I met in the circus taught me," he said. "We'd rent a car and go for rides in the country when we had free time."

Julie had no reply. She wondered how far the relationship between Stephen and this woman had progressed.

She nosed her midsize Ford into the traffic on U.S. 41. "What brought you down here to meet me?" she asked Stephen. She felt uncomfortable with him sitting in her car, his arm so casually draped over the armrest, his other hand resting lightly on one knee. There was something arresting about his very presence.

"I wanted to see you. What else?"

She eyed him suspiciously.

"You haven't asked me to join the Amazing Andrassys on the high wire, and we've been together ten whole minutes. That's a record."

"Have you changed your mind?"

"No."

He looked crestfallen. "That's too bad."

"The others are still with you?"

"Yes. I had hoped you would be, too."

She shook her head so vigorously that her long ponytail dusted both shoulders. "It's still no, Stephen. But tell me, when do you start practicing?"

"Next week. It is all arranged. I leave tomorrow."

"Leave? You mean you're not staying in Venice?"

"Paul has offered the use of his farm. So we are all going there."

"But that's in Georgia!" Julie was astonished at this news. She had supposed that the Andrassys would train here, in Venice, where so many circus acts practiced. She had not dreamed that they would leave.

"Financially it is the only way. His wife Carol has welcomed us. They have a big farmhouse with several bedrooms, and a barn that they are not using but that we can use for practice. There is a trailer on the farm, where Michael can live with his family. Paul does not want to be part of our act, but he wants to help the rest of us."

"I—I'm surprised," was all she could say. A truck horn blared behind her, and she switched lanes so that the truck could pass. All she could think of was that Stephen—and the others, of course—would be leaving.

"Nonna wants to go with us, Juliana."

"*What*! That's impossible!"

"But it is what she wants. After all, this is a family reunion of sorts. The only Andrassy who will not be there is Béla. And I want to make it possible for Nonna to go."

"Nonna isn't well! Her blood pressure—I have to remind her to take her medicine! And—"

"She could go if you went along to help her," he said quietly.

Julie turned her car down the peaceful palm-lined residential street where she and Nonna lived.

"I can't," she said firmly. "I have my job."

"Do you not have a vacation soon? Nonna said you do. She said you had suggested taking her somewhere this summer, somewhere she would like to go."

Not long ago, Julie *had* suggested a vacation to a destination of Nonna's choosing, thinking that it would be good for Nonna to get out of the house and have a good time. But to travel to someplace in rural Georgia—that was not what she'd had in mind. She'd thought about taking Nonna to Key West, where Nonna had friends. She'd thought Nonna might enjoy a summer-bargain four-day cruise to the Yucatán Peninsula in Mexico, and they could catch a cruise ship right out of Tampa. But rural Georgia?

She eased her car into the driveway and switched off the engine.

"Stephen," she said wearily, "you haven't been in town twenty-four hours yet, and you're already stirring up trouble."

"I wish you wouldn't look at it that way," he said unhappily.

Julie got out of her car and slammed the door hard. "Well, I do," she retorted, hurrying up the driveway to the house.

Nonna met her at the door, all smiles. She reminded Julie of nothing so much as a little brown wren chirping and fluffing her feathers. "Did Stephen tell you?" she asked excitedly. "Did he tell you that he wants me to go with him and the others to Paul's farm?"

"Nonna," Julie said as gently as she could, "you can't go alone. And I have to work."

Nonna's face fell pathetically. "But I do want to go. I have not seen my family all together in so long."

Stephen loomed behind Julie. "If Julie does not go along, I'm afraid it's not possible, Nonna. The rest of us must spend long hours working on the wire. We might forget to remind you to take your medicine, or—"

Nonna sniffed. "I am just an old lady that no one has time for," she said, burying her face in her hands. She seemed to deflate before Julie's eyes.

"Nonna, that isn't true," Julie said, her throat tightening.

"Yes, it is. For so long I have dreamed of having my family around me again, and now I cannot go. I might as well be dead."

Stephen lifted his shoulders expressively.

"But, Nonna," Julie pleaded, feeling as if the world were ganging up on her. She didn't want to go. She wasn't sure she was emotionally ready to be with so many Andrassys. They hadn't all been together since the accident.

"You said we could go anywhere I wanted to go on a vacation this summer," Nonna said, letting her hands fall away so that Julie could see her face crumpling like a paper bag. "And I want to go to Paul's farm. It is mean of you not to take me."

"I thought you'd want to go to Key West, or on a cruise, or someplace nice," Julie said desperately. "I didn't think you would want to go to Peaceable Kingdom, Georgia, for pity's sake." Thank goodness, Nonna hid her face in her hands again. Julie couldn't stand her disappointed expression.

"If only I could go to Georgia for a little while," Nonna said, with a surreptitious peek through her fingers to see what effect she was having on her granddaughter. "If only I could go for a week or two."

Julie saw the peek through the fingers, but she wasn't strong enough to avoid being manipulated by this crafty woman. What if she refused to go with Nonna, and then Nonna *did* die without ever seeing her family together again? What if they didn't go, and Nonna made her life miserable forever afterward, blaming Julie because it was all her fault that Nonna had missed this longed-for reunion?

Julie sighed. Years ago, she had made Nonna her responsibility. It appeared that there was to be no shirking that responsibility now.

"Tomorrow I'll ask my boss if he can spare me for a couple of weeks," she said in weary resignation.

Nonna's dejection faded miraculously in two seconds.

"That is what I hoped you would do," she said.

"And I, too," Stephen said, daring to look hopeful.

PEACEABLE KINGDOM, Georgia, lies northeast of Atlanta and is typical of small southern towns. It's the county seat, which means that a red-brick white-pillared courthouse sits smack in the middle of town, surrounded by a courthouse square where various town characters shelter under the tall, leafy trees in summer and comment on the passing parade.

One of the things they found to jaw about that summer was the Andrassy family.

"You reckon them folks is Gypsies?" one old geezer said to another after Albert Andrassy came out of the

Lion & Lamb Grocery carrying a big watermelon, put it in the trunk of his car and drove away.

The second man took time to transfer his tobacco from one cheek to the other.

"Reckon they might be," he allowed. "They's so dark-colored and all."

"One of 'em ain't," piped up another. "He got yellow hair. Yellow as I dunno what."

"I hear they got this big wire strung up out there at Carol Murchison's place."

"You mean Carol Andrassy."

"Well, Carol Murchison that *was*."

"Old man Murchison be spinning in his grave if he knew a bunch of Gypsies was camped out on his dairy farm."

"Camped out? They living in her house!"

"You don't say."

"And like I said, they got this big wire strung out across the far meadow. It's tall-like."

"Weren't that yellow-haired guy some kind of tightrope walker?"

"Sure was. In some kind of carnival or somethin'."

"Mmm-*mmm*! I declare. A bunch of Gypsies is settin' up to walk a tightrope across old man Murchison's meadow! What is the world comin' to, I wonder?"

They settled down to contemplate that and other such important questions while somebody slapped a checkerboard down on a sawed-off nail keg, and somebody else dug the checkers out of the pocket of his denim overalls.

Life would go on as usual in Peaceable Kingdom, Georgia.

AT ABOUT THE TIME Junior Bodine was capturing Bobby Joe Cabbagestalk's last king, Julie drove her blue Ford sedan onto the straggly main street in the town of Peaceable Kingdom.

"Which way now, Nonna?" she asked anxiously, seeing the town's only stoplight looming up ahead.

"Left, I think. No, right. Oh, I don't know. I don't see so well these days."

"Let me see the map," Eva said, peering over the back of the front seat. She studied the lines. "Looks to me like you turn right, Julie."

Julie negotiated the turn, then glanced in the rearview mirror. "Where do I go now?"

"You drive about five miles out of Peaceable Kingdom, then look for a subdivision called Andrassy Acres. And another mile down the road we'll see a rural mailbox with 'Andrassy' printed on it."

"Nonna, are you all right?" Julie asked anxiously.

"Of course I am all right. I'm going to see my family together again." Nonna smiled, and her eyes sparkled behind her glasses.

They passed Andrassy Acres, a development of nice-size brick houses on wooded plots of land. Eva craned her neck to look.

"It's a pretty subdivision," she commented, facing front again.

"It was smart of Paul," Julie said, "to think of selling off Carol's cows and dividing the land up for building houses."

"He had a bit of luck, too," Eva reminded her. "If it hadn't been for that new semiconductor plant starting up about ten miles from here, there wouldn't have been a market for the lots."

"Still, he's one Andrassy who has found a way to make a living without risking his neck on the wire every day," said Julie, unable to resist saying it.

"Oh, look," Eva said, eager to divert any argument with Julie about the wisdom of her own decision to go back on the wire. "There's the mailbox. See, it says 'Andrassy.'"

The driveway to the house was long and curving, and it wound through gently rolling hills dotted with trees. It was hot in midafternoon, and the air was humid. Grasshoppers sprang out of the way of the car, and cicadas buzzed in the underbrush. Soon they saw in front of them a two-story house of time-blurred brick.

"This is it!" Eva said excitedly.

Julie never had time to worry about the reunion being awkward. They were caught up in the outpouring of people from the house: Paul, swarthy and heavyset, and Carol, his wife, little and bursting with energy and excitement; bearded Albert, walking slowly along the dirt path from the barn; handsome, curly-haired Michael and his red-haired wife, Linda, with their children, Tonia and Mickey; and little Susan, the youngest cousin, shorn of her long pigtails and all grown-up at twenty.

And finally, when Julie thought that he wasn't there, Stephen appeared suddenly.

He had been down in the meadow testing the cable. When, on his way back, he heard the popping of gravel under the tires of the car, he had broken into a run, hoping that it really was Julie. As the car passed the path through the woods he saw Julie's profile, and he felt drenched with happiness. He had been so afraid that she would decide not to come, after all.

Julie stepped out of the car, tossing her long ponytail back from her face in a characteristic gesture. She laughed at something Albert said, and the melodious strain of her laughter tumbled through the air. Stephen hurried toward her.

"Let me help you with that," Stephen said, moving to take Julie's makeup case from her hand.

"No, I can—"

"Juliana," he said teasingly, "you must learn to give in once in a while."

She was so glad to see him again! "On little things," she said, letting the handle of the case slip from her hand to his. "Only on little things."

He grinned at her. "That is a start, at least."

Carol led them all into the house to show them where they would stay. Nonna's room was the small unused downstairs study, furnished for her visit with a bed so that she wouldn't have to climb the stairs. Eva, Julie and Susan were to share a blue upstairs bedroom with curtains of dotted swiss billowing languidly inward from the windows.

"Such a pretty room!" Julie told Carol, liking the view of trees and gentle hills beyond the curtains.

"Do you like it? I'm so glad! I washed the curtains just for your visit, and I made the bedspread myself." Carol whirled around the room, adjusting the height of the window sash, flicking an imaginary speck of dust off the dressing table. Julie had forgotten how Paul's wife fairly sparkled; her warmth and enthusiasm made seeing all the Andrassys together again easier than Julie had expected.

Nothing would do but that they must see the rest of the house, and so they stopped by the bedroom where Albert bunked in with Carol's two teenage sons—

Sam, who was working that day, and Eric, who was away at summer camp. They peeked briefly into Carol's snug sewing room that served Stephen as an office and was where he slept alone on the couch. They saw the big corner room that was Carol and Paul's master bedroom. Then they trooped out to the field where Michael was staying with his family in a two-bedroom trailer that had once been occupied by the foreman of the dairy, but was no longer in use, since most of the farm had been subdivided into tracts.

"There's cold watermelon on the back porch," Carol announced after they had finished their tour, and they gathered to rock in slat-backed rockers and to cheer on Michael's two children, who engaged in an impromptu watermelon-seed-spitting contest.

Stephen sat on the floor beside Julie's chair, eating watermelon for the first time. He wasn't sure if he liked watermelon or not; there were so many seeds! But he did like sitting beside Julie and listening to her talk about the long drive from Venice to Peaceable Kingdom with Nonna and Eva, liking the way she laughed about the lunch they had eaten in an awful fast-food restaurant along the way.

Finally, when they had all talked themselves out and the children had run away to catch grasshoppers to put in a jar, the talk died down and they sat, too lazy to move, inhaling the scent of roses, which were the shade of garnets, and watching white clouds sail slowly across a sky of brilliant sun-washed blue.

Nonna rocked gently in the shade of a wisteria vine, her face peaceful. "All my grandchildren are here," she murmured softly. "And my great-grandchildren, too. Oh, Julie, I am so happy."

And in that moment, Julie was happy for her.

Still, she had a feeling that it was going to be a long two weeks. The Amazing Andrassys would begin training on the wire tomorrow.

Chapter Four

The next day promised to be flawless, with white clouds like paper cutouts pasted against a pale blue sky. Stephen went to the meadow early, whistling as he walked. The grass beneath his feet was trampled in whorls on the path he had made with his constant walking back and forth in the past couple of days. Today he felt happy and buoyant. It was the day he had anticipated for so long.

He began to check the cable that he had strung between two trees. He concentrated so completely on his task that he was surprised to see a figure working its way toward him, not on the path he had made, but through the tall grass. He continued with his task. This was not the high wire; this was only a short cable strung three feet off the ground for practice, but it was important nevertheless.

Julie approached quietly, and at first he thought she was Eva. But then he saw the long ponytail bouncing around her shoulders. *Juliana,* he thought. He kept pulling the metal eye toward the hoist hook, finally fastening it. He didn't want to scare her away.

"You're out early," she said, standing in long grass that reached her knees. She wore a pair of light gray shorts and a shirt.

"So are you," he said. He ran a cloth over the cable.

"Want me to help?" she asked suddenly and unexpectedly.

He looked up. "You know what I'm doing?"

"You're looking for kinks," she said.

He tore off a piece of the cloth and tossed it to her. "You start at that end of the wire, and I will start at this end." His hair looked flaxen-gold with the morning sunbeams sparkling on it.

She nodded and began to wipe her bit of cloth along the cable.

"I saw Grandfather Anton and my father and Uncle Béla do this many times," she said by way of explanation. "It's important to check for meat hooks." Meat hooks were broken wires that could stick up and do damage to an unaware wire walker's foot.

"Yes," Stephen said. "This is old wire. And if there are any bumps or meat hooks, no matter how tiny, it could be dangerous."

"Where did you get the wire?" she asked.

"Paul had it. He kept it here on the farm, lying in those weeds over there. Putting it outdoors is the best way to age a cable."

"I didn't know Paul thought that there would ever be an Amazing Andrassy act again."

"He didn't. He just figured that in case it happened, it would be good to have aged wire. Now let's switch sides, and you rub your cloth the other way. It is best to double check each other."

Julie concentrated on her task. This looked like good, sturdy wire, and due to its outdoor aging, there seemed to be no grease left in it. She knew that steel cable is greased during the manufacturing process, and that such grease must be removed before the wire walker attempts to use that cable. It is possible to clean the grease off new wire by rubbing the wire until no grease appears; however, sometimes grease lurks inside the cable, not spilling out until the wire has been stretched for a time. The Andrassys always used cable aged in the out-of-doors because it was the safest.

"Now," Stephen said with satisfaction, "we are ready."

"I thought you were going to practice in the barn," she said, wondering why, if that was so, Stephen had stretched this cable between two trees.

"Later," Stephen said. "First I want to begin outdoors. I want us all to feel the fresh air, to breathe it, to become one with nature. If we become one with nature, then it is easier to conquer the strongest force of nature—gravity. Do you not believe this?"

"I don't think about it," Julie said shortly. She turned to walk away on the track of beaten grass.

"Juliana," Stephen said in a low tone. He blocked her way, standing there in blue jeans and a yellow T-shirt with the sleeves torn out. The shirt didn't cover his stomach, but was cut off to reveal the tight, hard muscles there.

"I want to explain something to you. I want you to understand why I have brought your family here for this."

She stared at him mutely, wishing he would move aside so she could pass.

"A cable in the air connects two points in space," Stephen said. "If I walk the cable, then I am the connector. I am the person who makes those two points in space one."

She was caught up in his intensity, in his purpose. It was clear that he believed wholeheartedly in what he was saying.

"There are spaces to be connected," he went on, his eyes glowing with the passion of his ideas. "Spaces to be connected between members of the Andrassy family before they can be as close as they were in the old days. When the Andrassy family again performs together on the high wire, they will no longer be apart in loneliness. Do you understand?"

She understood. She knew that he believed himself to be the instrument for reuniting her family. He was not only the walker of the real wire, but the walker of the invisible thread of communication he had unreeled for the Andrassys.

But for Julie, nothing was worth the risk.

"You are much too idealistic, Stephen," she said tersely. "There is nothing mystical about walking the high wire. It isn't an exercise of the spirit, but of the flesh. And the flesh is all too frail."

He wasn't fooled; he knew that she understood the point he had been trying to make. He felt pity for her. She looked so forlorn, so unhappy.

He reached out in sympathy and touched her shoulder. He wanted desperately to take her in his arms, to comfort her in a way that would drive the bad memories from her mind.

She stared up at him, momentarily distracted. Her lips were slightly parted, and her eyes were wide and shaded by richly fringed black lashes. He thought she was lovely.

"Oh, Juliana," he said, and he could not stop himself from inclining his head downward until their lips met in a kiss so soft and gentle that it might have been the wind brushing her lips and not a kiss at all.

And then she was gone, dodging through the tall grass, her ponytail bobbing behind her.

One thing was sure, Stephen thought regretfully. He could not allow himself to be distracted, to feel the desire that even now coursed through his veins as he watched her running in hasty retreat.

This was not the right time to become obsessed with Juliana Andrassy. He must remain a man of solitude.

Now and for the next three months he must concentrate on the wire, on himself in relation to it, and on combining the talents of all the other Andrassys into one integrated high-wire act.

"OOH," SUSAN SAID, closing her eyes. "I had no idea my shoulders were so tense."

Julie massaged her cousin's tight muscles slowly. She often performed this service for her gymnastics students.

"I'm next," Albert said. "Julie, you look like you know what you're doing."

"I've had lots of experience," Julie said easily. She was relaxing on the front porch after dark with her cousins after their first full day of practice.

"Did you see the way Stephen leaps onto the wire?" Sam, Carol's son, had spent the late afternoon watching them. He had trekked back from the meadow with the others in the early twilight, full of excitement and praise.

Albert chuckled. "The man's a genius," he said. He was perched on the porch railing, drinking a glass of lemonade.

"I could learn just from watching him," contributed Eva.

"But watch him we're not allowed to do. We must work, work until we think we can't go on, and then work some more." Michael rocked in a wicker rocking chair.

"Does that disturb you?" Eva wanted to know.

"No. He's right."

"Who is right?" Stephen asked. He appeared from the direction of the meadow, striding out of the darkness like a man with a mission.

"Oh, Stephen, you startled me," said Eva, who had almost jumped from her chair at his words. "We were just saying that you are right to make us work so hard."

The lamplight from inside the house cast a shimmering path on Stephen's blond hair.

"And we will work hard tomorrow, also. I was just in the meadow checking the king poles. Albert will go up on them in the morning."

"In the morning!" Susan said, startled. The king poles were rigged so that the wire was thirty feet off the ground. And it was a point of honor among wire walkers not to use a net.

"Yes," Stephen said, unperturbed. "Albert has not forgotten any of what he learned so many years ago. Have you, Albert?"

"No," Albert admitted. "Although I tried for a long time to deny that part of me. Still, it comes back to me. Like riding a bicycle. You know, they say you never forget how."

"That is true," Stephen said. He watched Julie as she left Susan and moved to stand behind Albert. Albert's shoulder muscles were taut; Julie massaged gently in her expert way.

Eva sighed. "It felt good on the wire today, Stephen," she said, tilting her head back and staring at the starry sky. "It was a homecoming of sorts."

"I am glad you feel that way." Stephen leaned against the side of the house, his arms crossed across his chest. The night was alive with the distant strain of crickets; a full moon floated above the trees. The heavy scent of gardenias blew in the air. He watched Julie as she massaged Albert's shoulders. She was intent on her task, her upper lip tucked beneath her bottom one, unaware that he observed her.

"Anyone want more lemonade?" Susan asked, standing up.

"I do," Michael said, handing her his glass.

"I would like some," Stephen said.

"I think I'll turn in," said Eva, who always required more sleep than anyone else. She stifled a yawn.

"Me, too," said Albert.

The two of them went inside. Susan returned with two glasses of lemonade, then decided to join Carol, Nonna and Paul in front of the television set in the living room.

"How about massaging my neck?" Michael asked Julie. She took her place behind him, her small-breasted figure silhouetted against the moonlit porch column. Stephen resolutely turned his eyes away.

"Stephen, do you think I could try getting up on the wire sometime?" This question was from Sam.

"Certainly. If your parents don't mind."

"Paul said it was okay. Mom has her doubts, but I can make her see it my way."

"Sam, you won't be able to go on the wire during the day when the others are practicing, because you'll be at work," Julie pointed out. "And you can't go up on the wire when no one is around. It wouldn't be safe."

"My job at the peach orchard will be over as soon as the crop's harvested," Sam argued. "That'll be about the first week in July."

Julie sighed in exasperation. It was bad enough to have to go on the high wire because you were an Andrassy. But Sam was Carol's son by her first marriage, and he had no need to uphold family tradition. The way Julie saw it, his leaning toward wire walking should under no circumstances be encouraged.

Michael set down his lemonade glass. "Thanks, Julie. I'd better go. It's time to read my kids their bedtime story." He stood, stretched, and hurried off in the direction of the trailer.

"Guess I'll go see what's on TV," Sam said. He disappeared inside the house. This left Stephen and Julie facing each other from opposite corners of the porch, squared off like boxing opponents.

"So," Julie said bitterly when she was sure Sam couldn't hear. "You're recruiting a new generation of wire walkers."

Stephen brought the lemonade to his lips with a light tinkle of ice cubes against glass. She watched the muscles in his throat work as he swallowed a long draft of the liquid. She inhaled a deep breath and tried to ignore the hollow feeling in her stomach.

"Sam asked about it. Of course, I will talk with Carol and Paul and find out if they object." Casually he set the glass down on a low table.

Julie walked to the end of the porch. Here the shadows were dense; the bright moonlight could not penetrate the thick ropes of wisteria climbing the porch columns. She cupped her elbows in the palms of her hands and shivered.

"You are not cold, are you, Juliana?" Stephen's rich voice was close behind her.

She shook her head.

"What is wrong then?"

At first she wasn't going to tell him. But then she thought, *why not?* He had barged into her life, a life that ran smoothly, and he'd turned it inside out. He had evoked emotions that she had not felt in years; he had unearthed unhappy memories that were best left buried. Why should he not know what pain he caused her? Why should he be allowed to think that he was as wonderful as all the other Andrassys told him he was?

Resentment, already deeply rooted, grew and blossomed into bitter words.

"You are what is wrong, Stephen."

"Juliana. How I wish that you would understand." His voice vibrated somewhere in the vicinity of her ear. It was a melodious voice, a smooth counterpoint to the jagged emotions in her heart.

"They're losing their fear," she said helplessly. "I can see it. Their fear was the only thing that kept them off the wire."

"So? It is good that they lose their fear. They cannot walk the wire in fear."

"Eva, for instance. She was so afraid. For years she wouldn't even go into an elevator, do you know that?

Well, she got over it. But to get her on the high wire! How did you do it, Stephen? How did you persuade someone like Eva to lose her fear?'' Julie was almost crying now, sobbing out her own fear.

"Eva decided for herself. The others did, also. You know that." He wanted to touch her, to alleviate her abject misery. But now *he* was afraid. Afraid that Julie would not find it in her heart to forgive him.

"Do you know how I'm going to feel, Stephen, when I know you're all down there in the meadow practicing on the high wire? Do you think I want to lose the rest of my family, too?" The words tore out of her, ripping at her heart.

"You must not worry. I have taken every care with the rigging. I am a professional, Juliana. Nothing will happen to any of us because we are very careful."

Julie's heart hammered in her chest. Dammed-up tears made her eyes ache; where could she go to cry? There was no privacy in this house, no privacy for her grief.

Blindly she whirled and ran down the steps, oblivious of Stephen's shouts. She headed for the driveway, not sure where she was going, but knowing that she needed to be alone.

But Stephen wasn't about to let her be alone. Guilt overwhelmed him. Julie was angry, sad, upset—and all because of him. Somehow he had to set things right with her.

He caught up with her as she was fumbling with the latch on a chained gate that led to one of the old unused pastures. The moonlight made everything almost as clear as day. He could see her features clearly, could discern her expression of anguish.

"Go away!" she demanded, tearing a fingernail on the stubborn latch. It ripped close to the quick, adding physical pain to her mental pain.

"Here, I will unlatch the chain if you will let go," Stephen said. He was so calm, so authoritative. With eyes glazed with tears, she stepped back. He didn't question where she was going, and she was glad of that because she didn't know.

"There," Stephen said. The gate pushed open with a swish against the high grass.

Uncertainly she passed through. She gripped her hurt finger tightly with the other hand.

"Now, where are we going?"

"I—I wanted to be alone."

He refused to acknowledge this. "We can walk this way," he said, gesturing toward a stand of trees. "There is a small brook there."

A soft wind soughed in the branches of the trees. Leaves rubbed together with a leathery sound, and little fruit bats swooped and dipped overhead. Something scurried through the tall grass, and Julie wondered what kind of night creature it was. Even though the moonlight illuminated the pasture well, Julie had to admit that she wouldn't have wanted to be alone there, after all. It was unfamiliar territory. She had been a fool to run off without so much as a flashlight.

When she didn't speak, Stephen said easily, "I have explored the farm, you know, when I was looking for the best place to set up the low practice wire and the king poles. The brook is very pretty, and I have always wanted to see it by moonlight."

He was probably lying, Julie reflected. He was just being courteous because he didn't think it would be right to abandon her out here all by herself. What an idiot she was! She couldn't give up and walk back to the house; she'd have to accompany him for a little while simply to save face.

She walked slightly slower than he did, a half-step behind. With a questioning smile on his face, he turned to her and slowed his step so that she walked beside him. His handsome features were silvered by the light of a moon as white as a magnolia blossom.

"Hear the brook?" he asked.

Julie nodded, still gripping her injured finger in her other hand. The lyrical sound of the rush of water over rocks grew louder as they approached.

"Watch your step here," Stephen cautioned, gripping her elbow. "There are many slippery rocks." The rocks, dampened by a diaphanous mist rising from the water, were indeed slippery. Once Julie grabbed Stephen's hand with a little cry.

"Are you all right?" he asked.

"Yes," she whispered. She wished she had never started this. When she'd felt her uncontrollable urge to burst into tears, she should have gone in the house as any sane person would have done. It would have been better to lock herself in the bathroom if she wanted to cry alone.

"Now," Stephen said when they stopped on the creek bank. The water swirled below them in graceful patterns, a froth of blue-white in the light from the moon. He reached into his back pocket and pulled out the rag with which he had wiped the wire this morning. "You may sit on this, so that your clothes will not get dirty from the rock." He spread the cloth out on a large flat rock and settled himself beside her.

The pearl-gray vapor rose from the stream, lending the moon-flooded creek bank a sense of unreality.

Damp sand edged the water, and little saplings dipped low on the other side of it, looking like the acrobats of the tree family. The water purled softly at their feet, singing a song of bewitchery, of moon-haunting in the mist. Julie sat down and put her finger with the torn fingernail in her mouth. She tasted blood.

He saw the flicker of pain cross her face.

"Is something wrong? he asked quickly. "Have you hurt your finger?"

Julie removed her finger from her mouth and inspected the fingernail. "I tore the fingernail off when I was trying to get the gate open," she explained. Here in the shadows at the edge of the creek the brilliant moonlight was muted, soft. She held out her finger to look at it.

"Here, we will wash it with the water of the brook," Stephen said. He stood up and bent over with a lithe movement. Smooth muscles rippled in his back, and his biceps flexed as he reached toward the water. He dampened his handkerchief in the swiftly running water and returned to her. He lifted her hand gently in his and dabbed at her fingernail.

"Does that make it feel better?"

Numbly she nodded, but the truth was that her hurting finger now seemed of secondary importance. At his touch she felt a flush spread throughout her body, and she was conscious of the soft sibilance of his breathing over the sound of the water. Her heart spread wide, filling up her chest and pulsing in her ears until she couldn't hear herself think. Stephen's chest rose and fell in her line of vision, a part of his strong, graceful, perfect body, so close that she could reach out and touch it if she wanted to.

Her hand in his quivered at the thought, and he darted a quick glance at her face. He seemed not to notice anything amiss there, and she bit down on her lip, trying to marshal her thoughts and pull them away from this man—this handsome, kind and talented man who openly admired her, who obviously enjoyed her company, and who cared enough about her not to let her wander at night in unfamiliar territory.

He tossed the handkerchief aside and resumed his position beside her, holding fast to her hand. She was too overwhelmed by his virile presence to object. From the corner of her eye she could see his sharp, straight nose, the dim shading of his light beard sweeping from sideburn to jaw, the thoughtful set of his generous lips. Her senses seemed sharpened, her body throbbed with electricity and her brain seemed to have become inoperative. She tried to swallow, only to discover that her throat was too dry.

"I have not been alone with many women since I came to the United States," he said slowly. "I am afraid that I don't know how to act." A smile touched the corners of his mouth, and he turned his head and focused his warm eyes upon hers.

She was trembling like a teenager at the thought of being so close to him, and he was going to talk about his love life? She tried not to show the dismay she felt.

"I don't think I know how to go about having what you call a relationship," he said softly, continuing to look at her.

"Stephen, I—"

"No, no, do not worry, Juliana. I only want to talk for a while." He laced his fingers through hers with a sigh. "To talk and feel close to another human being who knows me. Although I have always felt close to the Andrassys, I left all my friends behind when I left the Moscow Circus. There is no one here who knows me well, who understands my moods, who realizes what made me the person I am."

"Have you been so lonely?" Julie asked carefully, surprised that he was revealing so much of himself to her. Stephen had always seemed so self-sufficient and assured.

"Not entirely lonely. But yes, it is good for a man—or a woman—to have people who can be depended on to be a friend. I miss knowing the kind of person who would mourn if I had a pet that died, the kind of person I could call at three in the morning if I had a problem, the kind of person to whom I could reveal anything and who would not judge. Do you know what I mean?"

"Yes," Julie said. "A best friend."

"Is that what it is called? Yes, then I must mean a best friend." His voice was low, contemplative.

She had never considered the emotional wrench Stephen must have felt at leaving everything behind when he defected. His loneliness touched her; she felt a blossoming empathy.

"Did you have such a friend?" she ventured.

"Yes, he was a clown with the Moscow Circus. We were chums—er, best friends. He was married and his wife was my friend, too."

Julie thought she would not be able to say the words, but somehow she managed. "Did you have a special woman friend?"

"Oh, several. But not the kind you are thinking of. I did not have a lover. There were women over the years, but never anyone of long standing or who had

had any particular meaning in my life. And you, Juliana, surely you have had relationships?"

His openness made it easy for her to confide. "Once, long ago, I loved a man," she admitted. "It was after the accident, when I tried a lot of new and different things, frantically hoping to make sense of what had happened. His name was Andrew, and it lasted almost a year, but we simply weren't right for each other and I broke it off. I don't like to talk about it."

"No one since then?"

"No one. I had Nonna to take care of, and I had my work, and it was enough."

"You appointed yourself to take care of Nonna? Or the others expected you to? How did it happen that you are solely responsible for her, Juliana?" His voice was soft, seductive.

"I had to, it was my fau—" Horrified at what she had almost said, Julie yanked her hand from his. She tried to scramble to her feet, but her heel slipped on the mossy rock and she landed with a thud.

"What, Juliana, what were you going to say?" Stephen's intent face, damp with mist, loomed in her field of vision, so close that his riveting blue eyes were only inches from hers.

"Nothing, I wasn't going to say anything!"

His eyes held hers for interminable seconds until he suddenly relaxed and drew away. He clasped his hands loosely around his upraised knees and leaned his head back so that he could see the stars through the thin break in the tree branches above the creek bed. When she had slipped, she had been about to say something, something important. Suddenly he knew that there must be a key to Julie's fear—a key that would unlock her pent-up emotions.

Julie trembled violently beside him, unable to stop herself from shaking. She had let him get too close; she had almost said too much! How had he gained her trust in such a short period of time? How had he insinuated himself into her confidence? No one knew, *no one*, not even Eva, who was not only her cousin but her closest friend.

"Juliana, are you feeling cold?" Stephen said compassionately. "I will warm you for a moment." Tenderly he settled an arm around her shoulders, infusing her with the heat of his body. She didn't want him to see her face. He knew her too well, would read her thoughts, and so she buried her face in his sinewy shoulder, inhaling the new-mown hay scent of him, resting for only a moment, only a moment.

He lifted a hand and reflectively smoothed her ponytail back across her arm, reveling in the silkiness of it. She had beautiful hair—if only she would wear it down more often! He resisted an impulse to pull the band off and throw it in the creek. He knew that she would be appalled if he did. She would not only be furious, but he would also lose her confidence. And now more than ever he wanted to know her depths, to understand her, to find the key that would unlock her fear, to be her best friend.

When Julie finally lifted her head, Stephen was smiling, but there was something serious in his smile. Before she could define it, he said kindly, "Let us go, Juliana. You should not get a chill. But I would like to be with you sometimes like this, just the two of us. To be friends."

Silently she nodded, and he removed his arm. She shivered again, and she suddenly realized that the rock beneath her felt chill and hard. He helped her to her feet and tucked the cloth she had sat on back into his pocket.

"Follow me," he said, reaching a hand out for hers. "Put your feet in the exact same place I do, and you will not fall."

She did as he said, clinging tight to his strong, warm hand as they traversed the slippery rocks.

They emerged into the wide moonlit pasture, but Stephen did not release her hand until they reached the front porch of the house. The house was quiet and dark; only a single night-light burned at the head of the stairs.

"I am going to get something to eat from the kitchen," Stephen said when he had locked the front door behind them. "Would you care to join me?"

"No, Stephen. I'm very tired." Not the truth. Julie doubted that she would sleep at all tonight, so aroused were all her senses.

"Then I'll say good-night. Thank you, Juliana. I enjoyed being with you." His eyes were bright, and his voice was much too formal.

Julie could do no more than nod before she fled up the wide staircase. She crept into bed as quietly as she could, hoping that neither Eva nor Susan would awaken. She didn't want to have to explain what had happened between her and Stephen down at the creek.

She wasn't sure she even understood it herself.

Chapter Five

"Why don't you come down to the meadow and watch us sometime?" Albert asked Julie as they sat eating breakfast one day. "You'd be proud of how well we're doing."

"No thank you," Julie said primly.

"Who shall I call today—Hot Spa Incorporated or the Gabriel Clinic of Cosmetic Surgery?" Nonna mused, pouring over her directory of 800 numbers as she sat in a chair beside the wall telephone.

"I vote for Hot Spa Incorporated," Julie said.

"They will try to sell me a hot tub. Maybe they will offer a free trip to their display room to see it."

"You already won a free trip once. We had a heck of a time giving it back."

"Well, it's easier giving back a trip to Hot Spa Incorporated than a face lift, which is what I'm afraid I will get if I call the Gabriel Clinic."

"I thought you never bought anything," Carol commented, whizzing through the kitchen with her arms full of clean laundry.

"I don't, but what if they sign me up for something I cannot cancel?" Nonna worried. "There are supposed to be laws about canceling if you don't want what you've bought, but I don't know anything about them.''

"Maybe Carol and Paul don't like your using their phone for your hobby," Julie said when Carol was in the laundry room, out of hearing distance. Julie was sweeping the kitchen floor, which she did after breakfast every day.

"Oh, they don't mind," Nonna said comfortably. She tapped a finger thoughtfully on the page of the book. "You know," she said, "I really should call a number where they mail you a free catalog. It's so nice to get mail afterward. Do you suppose the Gabriel Clinic of Cosmetic Surgery has a catalog of new faces they can make?"

"Nonna, I can't imagine." Julie stowed the broom in the closet and pushed the button on the dishwasher. "There," she said, surveying the clean kitchen with pleasure. "All cleaned up."

"I'm late. Guess I'd better get on down to the meadow. 'Bye, Nonna." Albert drained his coffee cup and bent to kiss Nonna's withered cheek. Nonna smiled a beatific smile as he rushed out the back door, and Julie hurried upstairs to make beds before Nonna could start dialing.

Their days on the farm had settled into a peaceful routine. Everyone woke up early, and Carol, Nonna and Julie cooked a big breakfast. Then Stephen, Albert, Michael, Susan and Eva went to the meadow to practice. They usually broke for an hour-long lunch before going back to work. At dinnertime everyone gathered around the big oval dining room table, and talk revolved around the day's happenings on the wire.

"Eva is doing so well on her half turns. I would never guess that she had left the wire for eight years."

"I will never do a headstand on the cable without my balancing pole. It is simply not safe. It is—"

"Tomorrow I will attempt the forward roll over you and Eva and Susan. Soon I'll be ready to do a forward roll over four of you. Just give me time, a bit of time."

"We can't practice outside if it rains. That's why we need to set up the cable in the barn as soon as possible, Paul."

And on and on it went, every night, until Julie thought she couldn't stand it anymore.

The person who saved her was Carol. She seemed to be the only one of them with her feet anchored firmly on the ground. She didn't talk nonsense about walking the wire; in fact, she said very little. But she remained constantly cheerful, happy and upbeat.

"Doesn't it bother you, having all of us here?" Julie asked Carol curiously one day as they hung out sheets together on the long clothesline in back of the house.

"No, I love it." Carol smiled. "I've always hoped that someday Paul could have his family here all at once."

"It's good of you to have us," Julie said.

"I've never gotten used to staying home and being a housewife," Carol admitted, snapping clothespins onto the corners of wet linen with decisive clicks. "I'm a registered nurse, you know, and I always worked at the hospital. Paul thought I might like to stay home for a while, and so did I. But the boys are teenagers, and they're not around as much as they used to be. Paul's busy with his business. So it's been wonderful that you've all been here. I'll hate to see everyone go."

Carol and Julie planned the huge meals the family ate; they went into town and shopped. Through everything Carol remained unflappable, with more energy than even Julie could muster.

And Carol was so good with Nonna. She, along with Julie, helped Nonna remember when it was time to take her medicine. Carol even took Nonna's blood pressure once a day to make sure it was within normal limits. And she tolerated Nonna's unusual telephone hobby with amused indulgence.

They had been at the farm for almost a week. One more week to go, and then Julie and Nonna would leave. Julie faced their leave-taking with mixed feelings. She would have looked forward to it if it hadn't meant leaving Stephen. She was beginning to respect him and to see him in a different way.

It wasn't that Stephen had changed. Stephen remained intense and dedicated. When working on the wire, he pushed the others to the limits of their endurance and skill, never becoming overbearing or angry. His way was to cajole, to encourage, to teach. Never once did Julie hear any of them complain about Stephen becoming angry or disparaging. As a teacher of gymnastics, she grew to appreciate his sensitivity toward those who were learning from him.

Toward her, Stephen remained kind, interested and polite. Several times they had found themselves alone, and each time he charmed her with his ability to relate to the person she was. He did not see her as Julie, another Andrassy. He saw her as a gymnastics teacher, and he asked effortless questions about her work, her students and her hopes for Molly, the student with Olympic possibilities. He saw Julie as Nonna's granddaughter, concerned about her grandmother's health, and his astute comments told her that he understood the problems of taking care of a seventy-six-year-old woman with a heart ailment.

He saw her as a woman.

She divined his appreciation of her womanhood in the light warming his eyes as he smiled at her when he was sitting at the breakfast table in the early morning, with his supple fingers curved around a coffee mug. She understood his appreciation as expressed by the intimate angle of his body whenever he leaned toward her to talk. She sensed it in the sensual droop of his eyelids, the firm set of his chin, the full curve of his lips. She knew as a woman knows when a man is undeniably attracted to her.

She responded to his charm with an answering charm of her own. She couldn't help it; it just happened—the half-smile in answer to something he said when they were in a group, a brightness flaring momentarily in her eyes when he made a point that she understood better than anyone else, their sharing of that understanding in a glance that no one else would notice.

The subtle electricity flowed freely between them, an unseen bond that the others didn't detect. It carried thoughts, ideas, emotions—all unspoken, but no less real for all that. And the result of all this was that Julie felt incredibly energized, refreshed and renewed. After a few hours in Stephen's presence Julie felt imbued with his special force and vigor. It was sexual and yet not sexual, and Julie was at a loss to define it.

Stephen and the others customarily worked on the wire every day but Sunday. When their first Sunday at the farm rolled around, Susan declared her intention to take a long nap after their noonday Sunday meal.

Paul, Carol and Sam were scheduled to go to a wedding. Nonna and Albert became involved in an old Errol Flynn movie on television, and Michael's family went on an outing to Lake Lanier. Always a reader, Eva settled down with a thick paperback novel, and Julie decided that she would give herself a manicure and try to repair her torn fingernail.

Julie had just sat down in the swing under the grape arbor when Stephen approached. He was wearing a navy-blue polo shirt and khaki slacks; his hair rippled in the slight breeze as he strode toward her.

"I would like to go for a ride," he said, smiling down at her. His smile tugged at her heart, and for a moment she felt giddy.

"And since you have a car," he continued, "I thought maybe you would let me borrow it."

"Of course, Stephen," she said, her cool answer belying her tripping pulse. "The car keys are in my handbag on the coffee table in the living room." She opened the box of her nail-repair kit.

"Oh, but I don't want to go alone. I would like you to go with me."

"You're perfectly welcome to use my car," Julie said. "I don't mind."

He knelt beside her, toying whimsically with the rainbow-striped sash of her yellow voile sundress.

"You miss the point, Juliana. I want your company as much as I want the car. Now, will you please go get your handbag and come with me? Everyone else is busy with his or her own pursuits. No one will miss us for a few hours."

She stood up, unable, for some reason, to let him go on playing with her sash.

"Well, I—"

"I thought we'd drive about an hour to the north to a very scenic place. Do you mind?"

"The others might like to come," she babbled inanely. "Nonna—"

"Nonna is watching Errol Flynn leap from mast to mast of the pirate ship. Albert is popping popcorn for her. They are very happily established in front of the television and there will be no removing them. I mean *moving* them." He grinned at his own mistake, then resumed looking at Julie in happy anticipation. At that moment Julie realized that there was no point in refusing, because Stephen had no intention of taking no for an answer. Slowly she put the nail enamel back in the box and stood up.

"Where are we going?" Julie asked, aware of Stephen's hand in the middle of her back, propelling her gently toward the house.

"I'll tell you that once we get started."

"You're impossible," she said over her shoulder as she went inside. He only lifted his eyebrows to communicate his amusement.

"We are going to a place called the Tallulah Gorge," he told her once they were in the car. He was driving—"to show off my new accomplishment," he had said. He drove skillfully and well, although a trifle over the speed limit.

"What is it?"

"You don't know what is Tallulah Gorge?" he teased.

"No, I don't."

"Then I will tell you," he said, looking pleased. "Tallulah Gorge is the oldest natural chasm in the eastern part of North America."

"In Georgia?"

"In Georgia."

"Why do you want to go there?"

"Various reasons, not the least of which is the fact that as a future citizen of this country, I owe it to myself to see the sights. Not to mention the fact that I did not want to sit around on a lovely Sunday afternoon watching Errol Flynn saving well-endowed ladies from pirates."

Julie smiled at Stephen's eagerness and turned her eyes away to watch the scenery skimming past. It was a beautiful day; a few clouds trailed scarflike across the bright lucent blue of the sky. Waves of heat fluttered in the air above the highway. The day was hot, but Julie was dressed in her coolest sundress, and her car was air-conditioned.

The highway was a ribbon festooning a countryside quilted with shades of greenery. Trees in a peach orchard drooped laden boughs toward the ground, and two black-and-white ponies grazed in the shade of a hickory tree. Occasionally, leaves flickered green overhead, providing welcome relief from the hot sun.

"Look, I see mountains!" Julie said as they rounded a curve and hazy lavender peaks appeared in the distance.

"Take a look at the guidebook and tell me what it says about them," Stephen suggested. He handed her a small book and she opened it to the place he had marked.

" 'The Blue Ridge Mountains rise in the northeastern part of the state of Georgia,' " read Julie. " 'The height of the mountains varies from two thousand to five thousand feet above sea level.' "

"And the Tallulah Gorge is a thousand feet deep," Stephen said. He gripped the steering wheel as the car climbed a grade.

He was intent on his driving, but Julie slanted a look at him through her lashes, noticing the tangle of golden hair on the backs of his hands. What a dumb thing to notice, almost as dumb as the freckle on his earlobe. She turned her head away and made herself gaze out the window, although she didn't really see the scenery. She was aware of him beside her, of the taut fabric of his pants stretched across his muscular thighs, of the light blue tracing of veins on the inner part of his left forearm. Why was she always aware of the physical side of Stephen when she was near him? Was it because she was overaware of his strength, his power? Or was it more than that—a natural response to a man who was overwhelmingly attractive?

Uncomfortably she shifted in her seat; the blast of air from the air-conditioning vent caught the edge of her sheer skirt and billowed it upward, exposing her leg to midthigh. Julie tugged a handful of capricious voile over her knees.

"A shame," Stephen said in a teasing tone.

She flushed. "Stephen, I—"

"You have very pretty legs, Juliana," he told her with a jaunty tilt to his head. He was flirting with her.

She bit her lip, suddenly shy with him. He sensed her shyness, as he so often sensed things about her.

"If I have been too forward, you must tell me. But I never have understood why, if I have seen your legs when you wear shorts, as you do every day, you must pull your skirt down when it blows up."

Julie shrugged. "A quaint American custom," she said, struggling to inject a shred of humor into the situation.

Stephen's mouth curled at the corners. "I like it when you make jokes," he said. "As long as I understand them, that is."

The road twisted even more as they climbed the foothills, and soon sheer walls of rock hung with ferns and moss abutted the side of the road. They saw a sign with an arrow that pointed them in the direction of the Gorge, and it was with some curiosity that Julie stepped out of the car when they reached the Tallulah Point lookout.

"It's glorious!" Julie exclaimed, running to the low rock wall overlooking the chasm. "It's magnificent!"

The Gorge stretched out before them in all its grandeur. Cut through the rock by the mighty Tallulah River, its craggy sandstone walls were plumed with the green of hardy shrubs and trees. At the bottom Julie saw the river, mighty no more. According to the plaque on the wall, the Tallulah River with its six majestic waterfalls had been dammed and diverted through an underground tunnel by the Georgia Power Company in 1913.

With the river raging in its depths, the Gorge must have been magnificent. And with the river a mere trickle below, Tallulah Gorge was still a stupefying sight, staggering in its dimensions.

"I had no idea," Stephen breathed in wonder. "I didn't think it would be like this."

The wall on the far side of the Gorge seemed to bend toward them in an optical illusion. Julie blinked, trying to focus her eyes. But it was impossible.

"Why does it seem to move?" Stephen asked in an awed voice. "I don't understand."

"I don't know, but it's like a three-dimensional movie. Have you ever seen one?"

Stephen nodded. "Yes, I did, when I traveled to France one time with the circus. The effect of the Gorge is exactly like that. Come, let us see if there is a telescope inside the building."

A shelter housing a gift shop at one end stretched along the rim of the Gorge. On the open side of the shelter was a telescope. Stephen produced a quarter and inserted it into the slot. "You look first," he said. After Julie finished, he took his place behind the telescope. He whistled a long, low whistle. "It is hard to get my bearings with the Gorge seeming to bend back and forth like that. It must be some sort of visual trick that it plays."

Julie read more of the information printed on the plaque. "Why, Stephen," she said in surprise. "Two wire walkers have crossed the Gorge on cable."

"Mmm," Stephen said, continuing to gaze through the telescope.

"A Professor Leon walked a cable across the Gorge in 1886," she read. "And Karl Wallenda walked it in 1970. Did you know that?"

"I remember hearing something about it," Stephen said vaguely. She shot him a sharp look. He was training the telescope on a faraway mountain peak, so she returned her attention to the written information. "I would like to bring Nonna here sometime," she said.

Stephen straightened when his quarter ran out and the telescope clicked off. He flicked a quick glance in her direction. "Maybe you can someday," was all he said.

"There is one more thing I want to see while I am here," Stephen told her when they were back in her car. He idled slowly, looking for a turnoff. When he found it, they drove down a curving unpaved road leading to a cleared area, which turned out to be a rutted sand parking lot at the edge of the Gorge.

"You can wait in the car if you like," he said. "You don't have to get out."

"Where are you going?"

"Not far. Only to the edge of the cliff. I want to get a good look at the view."

"I think I'll stay here," she said. "I don't want to get sand in my sandals."

Stephen looked relieved. He got out of the car and strolled with his hands in his pockets to the edge of the parking area where the chasm yawned below.

Julie watched two children, there on a tailgate picnic with their parents. They had a new puppy, and it was running away with one of the children's socks. A brisk tug of war ensued, and Julie scarcely noticed the attention Stephen paid to a red-painted steel pylon on the far side of the family's station wagon. Nor did she notice his surreptitious glances toward the car to see if she were paying attention. He didn't take a long time to inspect the pylon. He didn't need to. He had found what he had come to find. Before Julie could change her mind about getting out of the car, he hurried back to her.

"Well, Juliana, now you have seen the Tallulah Gorge," Stephen said as he backed out of the parking spot and drove along the dirt road, stirring up a cloud of yellow dust. "Now I think we should find a restaurant and get something to eat."

"But it's not really late," she objected.

"It will be by the time we get to the restaurant," he reasoned. Julie sat back in her seat and stared out at the scenery. Since reading the plaques on the wall at Tallulah Point, she had other things on her mind.

The restaurant Stephen chose was a family-style inn a good twenty miles north of Tallulah Gorge. It rested in Rabun Gap and had existed since before the Civil War, when its proprietors had provided food and lodging for travelers crossing the Blue Ridge.

"How did you find this place?" Julie asked when they were seated and their plain oaken table was cluttered with piled-high plates of hearty country food. The restaurant was crowded with vacationers on holiday in the mountains.

"Paul told me about it," he said, watching her. Her cheeks were flushed, and her hair, loosened from its ponytail by the stiff breeze at the Gorge, ruffled around her face. The yellow sundress complemented her vivid coloring, and he thought she had never looked more beautiful.

Julie seemed somehow distracted, gazing out the window at the brick buildings of a school that adorned the hills on the other side of the road. The rapidly encroaching twilight dimmed the shapes of the mountain peaks in the distance; soon it would be dark.

"What's on your mind, Juliana?" Stephen asked. She was looking much too pensive in the atmosphere of food and conviviality that surrounded them.

"Just thinking," she said quickly.

"Now, Juliana," Stephen said reproachfully, setting his fork down and tapping her sharply but gently on the wrist. "You must stop that. This is supposed to be a good time for us."

"I keep thinking about those wire walkers crossing Tallulah Gorge. How difficult it must have been with the added problem of the optical illusion. And how lucky they were to have crossed it successfully."

A guardedness flashed into Stephen's eyes; then, just as quickly, it was gone. He helped himself to more mashed potatoes and poured cream gravy over them.

"Oh?" he said, communicating only mild interest.

"I wonder how they could have attempted it." She poked at her food, feeling more like talking than eating.

"It was their choice," Stephen said philosophically. "Would you like more corn? It is very good."

Julie waved the bowl of creamed corn away. "I respect their choice, their desire to practice their art. I just don't understand it."

"Well," Stephen said, momentarily at a loss for words.

"Maybe it's because I never had a choice," Julie said unhappily.

"What do you mean?" Stephen went on eating, but he sensed that this conversation was important to Julie. He was sure that she never talked about her feelings on the subject of the family profession to anyone else.

"It was expected. You know, you're born an Andrassy. So you're trained to go on the high wire. Period."

"I was not born an Andrassy, and I had a choice. My choice was to walk the wire. To defy nature, to entertain an audience with my daring—this seemed important and right."

"Oh, Stephen, it was different for you."

"I suppose it was," he said carefully.

"I've thought about it a lot," Julie went on in a low voice, "about being born an Andrassy and having so much expected of me. You know, maybe I would have made a good nurse. Taking care of Nonna makes me think I might have been. Or a chemist. Do you know that I was very good at chemistry in high school? I had the top marks in my class. Or—well, there are any number of things I might have done with my life." She spoke earnestly, her ebony eyes flashing.

Stephen's eyes registered understanding. "You do resent it, don't you?"

Julie nodded. "Seeing the rest of you go off to practice day after day has brought out so many emotions I'd buried for so long. Not just the fear, but the anger. I'm angry, Stephen! I'm furious that I had no choice in the matter!"

Stephen could not speak. Julie's emotion was genuine, and her outburst saddened him. He knew that she was right. She had never had a choice of being anything but one of the Amazing Andrassys.

He chose his words carefully. "Now I know why you hated me so when I tried to convince you to rejoin the act. Maybe you can get over these feelings, now that you've identified them. Do you think you can?" A frown line creased Stephen's forehead. He was worried about her.

"I never hated you, Stephen. Never!"

The way she said it, with such intensity, made his breath catch in his throat.

"You put up with me because of Nonna," he said.

"No, no." She shook her head vigorously. She couldn't bear it if he really thought that.

"Juliana, I have always been sorry to cause you pain. But now—now you have a choice. And you chose not to join us on the wire. So you see, everything is all right now."

Sudden tears blurred her eyes. All she could see was a sheaf of wheat-colored hair across the table and a pair of brilliant blue eyes that reflected sympathy, tenderness and understanding.

"Yes," she said slowly. "I suppose it is." She felt as though a burden had been lifted off her shoulders. Speaking of her anger and resentment had lightened her load. Still, she carried another load—one of guilt. And that, she knew, could never be lightened.

"I think," Stephen said, "that we have had enough to eat." For a brief moment, he looked as though he didn't merely want to look at her but wanted to consume her.

Julie blinked to clear the tears from her eyes and glanced down at her plate. With effort, she ignored the burgeoning sexual tension. "You've had enough to eat. I hardly ate a thing. And the food is delicious, too."

Surprised at the flutter of humor in her voice, Stephen smiled indulgently. "Finish your dinner, Juliana. I am in no hurry."

Julie ate, relaxing, enjoying his company. Several of the women passing their table let their eyes linger on Stephen longer than necessary, and Julie realized suddenly that she enjoyed being in the company of such a handsome man. She didn't date often. She didn't consider this time with Stephen an actual date. But she enjoyed being envied by other women who were impressed by Stephen's wholesome good looks.

After dinner they drove home slowly, feeling their closeness build as they rode along the winding country roads in the dark car. The space between them was static with unuttered feelings, unvoiced thoughts. They could have talked, could have filled the silence with words and phrases. But it didn't seem necessary. To be quiet together seemed entirely natural, as natural as it was now for them to feel comfortable baring their deepest feelings to one another.

Julie did not speak as Stephen turned the car into the driveway next to the mailbox that said "Andrassy." But her nerves felt strung tight, feeling anxious at not knowing what was going to happen next.

Stephen slowed the car at a curve, and before she knew it, he had turned out the lights and let the car glide to a stop beneath a tall oak tree. He cut the engine, and it was quiet except for the shrill song of insects in the undergrowth.

"Juliana, I—" Stephen removed his hands from the wheel and let them lie passively on his thighs while he collected his thoughts. What to say to her? What could he say that could express his feelings for her? She was, quite simply, the woman he loved. The woman he loved. The words throbbed in his eardrums, sounding strange but right. There had never been a woman whom he loved before.

He turned to her, and the world was in her eyes. They were dark, deep, the pupils wide. He had subconsciously steeled himself for her rejection, but now he knew there would be no rejection.

He reached toward her slowly, watching her expression. His finger touched her cheek gently. Her skin was soft, so soft. As soft as silk.

She was bending toward him as though unable to stop herself, her hands finding their way up his arms, past his collar, until they enclosed his face and she said, "Oh, Stephen." His lips found hers, covered them; she was moist and warm, her lips opening to his, and he kissed her as though he were a man deprived—which of course he was, a man deprived all his life of this Julie, this Juliana.

His muscles strained in the uncomfortable position until finally Julie pulled away and reached down to pull a lever which made the seat go back.

"That is better," he said, reaching for her again. Her arms went around him. "That's better, too," he told her approvingly before lowering his lips to hers.

Julie's dress rustled against the upholstery of the seat as she tried to find a more comfortable position.

"This is not good," Stephen said, releasing her lips. "My foot is going to sleep."

"My arm, too." Julie moved to tug her arm away, the one that was pinned between Stephen's side and the seat.

"But I do like kissing you," Stephen said, preparing to do it again.

Julie succumbed, helpless and weak with desire. His lips cooled the heat within her—no, made it worse—and she clung to him, swept with yearning. He was an expert at kissing, and his kisses were laced with a tantalizing tenderness. Then his lips pursued a breathy path to her throat, and she heard herself moan, sounding so far away. His light beard abraded her skin; he whispered her name as only he could say it, and she closed her eyes and focused on his lips, only his lips, while her hands swept upward and tangled in his silky hair. She pressed his head to her breast.

"Juliana," he said, and the syllables of her name breathed against her hot flesh became the instrument of her desire. "This is not the way I want this to happen. Cramped in your car, parked on the road to your cousin's house. Anyone could come along now, do you know that? Sam coming home from a date, Michael and his family on their way back from the lake."

Julie fought for control. Stephen was sitting up and pulling her up with him, nuzzling her cheek, wrapping his arms around her, holding her close. It felt so good to be held like that. But he was right.

"We can't stay here," she agreed, her voice trembling.

"So we must go. I cannot ruin your reputation with the family. You understand that, don't you?" He traced her eyebrow with his little finger and smiled at her in the darkness.

She leaned her forehead against his. "Maybe it's just as well. I need to think about this, Stephen. You have been my friend, but it would be different between us if you were my lover."

"I know." His eyes were serious under the pale brows. "It would change everything. Do you not want things to change for us, Juliana?"

"I like us the way we are," she answered truthfully, trying to ignore the passion that had been so easily ignited between them. "I like having someone I can talk to about the things I've never spoken about before. You do understand what I mean, don't you?" She searched his face anxiously, hoping that he wasn't taking her words as a rebuff.

"Yes, my Juliana. I understand." He intuitively sensed that Julie wasn't rejecting him as much as she was clinging to the hope that someday she might be able to speak the words that would unlock the pain she hid in her heart. When that day came, Stephen wanted to be the one in whom she confided. Securing her trust was the only way he knew to help her.

His voice was filled with caring. "We will go home now. And I think that we don't need to rush. Perhaps we need to back off a bit, no?" He started the engine.

She stopped his hand before he could throw the car into gear. "Thank you, Stephen," she said softly. "For being such a nice person." She leaned over and kissed him on the cheek.

He smiled fondly. "It is easy to be a nice person around you," he told her. She slid her hand into his and squeezed it companionably. He squeezed back. Her hand nestled inside his, as though it belonged to him, and there it stayed as Stephen drove slowly to the house.

Chapter Six

His concentration on his task was absolute; when Stephen Andrassy walked on a high wire, nothing intruded on his mind. This ability to concentrate was acquired, not a gift. And because he had worked so hard to learn to focus his very being on the cable, nothing but the cable, he treasured this skill above all others.

Below, the rest of the performing troupe watched, their faces upturned. They held their breath. Stephen Andrassy walked with pride and confidence. So, too, did they.

On the edge of his consciousness Stephen was aware of them, but only just aware. He became part of the wire. It swayed; he swayed. It lived for him, an entity unto itself. His mystical union with it, a model of classical perfection, was something few other human beings understood.

He leaped onto the platform with characteristic grace and ease as the group beneath him burst into applause.

"That," he said, calling down to them, "is the way it is to be done. With lightness. With concentration. Anytime you do not concentrate, you put the lives of your family at risk. If you cannot concentrate, you must not walk the wire. It is as simple—and as difficult—as that." He set his balancing pole carefully on the platform and nimbly descended the ladder.

"Now," he said, after a quick assessment of ominously dark clouds churning toward them, "we will take a break. It looks as though it is going to rain, and the rigging in the barn is not ready for us to practice there. We will meet again in the morning as usual."

The others, laughing and talking, hurried away as swiftly as children unexpectedly let out of school. Stephen lingered, adjusting a stake here, tugging at a guy line there. He licked a finger and held it up to test the wind. He didn't like the way it was gusting. He made a few more minor adjustments to the rigging, taking his time. He'd rather that the others went ahead to the house. He didn't feel like being with them for once. He wanted to think.

Distant thunder rumbled, shaking the ground. It was time to leave the meadow, before the rain came. He walked, head down, lost in thought.

Juliana would leave over the weekend. She had to go back to Venice and her job at the gym. And she was just beginning to trust him, too. That was the saddest part. Now that she finally talked freely to him, took him into her confidence, she was leaving.

He had tried so hard to build a friendship with her. And he had done that, even though he'd been afraid at first that she really didn't like him much. Now he knew that she liked him, and he was sure that he loved her. But his love would mean nothing to her if he told her about it now, in the aftermath of their passion the other night. He wanted her to understand that "love" was not a word he tossed around at random. With him, it was serious to love someone.

It could be many long months before he would have an opportunity to spend an extended time with her again. Would everything he had gained in the past week and a half be lost during that time? He thought it might. In his experience, absence didn't make the heart grow fonder. The opposite was true. All absence did was create fond memories, and he couldn't be satisfied to be nothing more than a fond memory to Juliana. He wanted, certainly, to be much more than that.

Little raindrops began to spatter his face, and he saw a heavy curtain of rain bearing down on him from the other side of the meadow. It was too late to reach the house before the storm. He set off at a jog for the nearest shelter, the barn.

The barn door was open and he ran inside. He was surprised to find someone else there.

"Stephen," Julie called from where she was sitting in a corner on the hay-covered floor. "It looks as though you're through practicing for the afternoon." Beside her, nestled in the hay, were Michael's two children—Mickey, who was six, and Tonia, who was four.

"Yes, I think the rain has cut our session short," Stephen said with a worried backward look at the roiling clouds. He had never seen clouds so black.

"We were picking flowers along the fence for the dinner table," Tonia said importantly. "We had to run in here when the storm came."

"I ran fastest," Mickey claimed. "I beat everyone."

Julie smiled up at Stephen. "Sit down and join us," she said. "It looks as though we're captives here until the storm passes."

Drops of rain bounced off the red dirt, making little explosions outside the barn door. Raindrops drummed on the metal roof. The barn smelled of fresh hay, which Stephen had ordered spread there so that the barn floor would be well-cushioned in case anyone fell during practice on the cable he was rigging high up under the roof.

He sat down with the little group and leaned back against the rough gray boards of the barn wall. From where they sat they could see outside, and the wind seemed to be growing in fury. Great sweeps of rain lunged at them through the open barn doors. Stephen would have closed them, but the double doors opened out. Anyway, the four of them were safe and snug in their corner.

"I wanna go back to the house," Mickey said after a particularly loud crack of thunder. "I don't like it here."

"I don't like it here, either," piped Tonia. Her brown eyes were round with fright.

"We can't go to the house yet, children," Stephen said kindly. He knew how they felt. He had been afraid of lightning and thunder himself once.

"Let's play a game," Julie said suddenly and enthusiastically.

"But I don't wanna play a game," Mickey complained.

"What game?" Tonia asked curiously. A dart of lightning split the sky, striking perilously close to them. Thunder followed immediately, shaking the barn to its foundations. Tonia began to wail, and Mickey's lips quivered.

"I think we should play a game, too," Stephen said quickly, with a conspiratorial look at Julie. He knew that she was trying to distract the children.

"Good," Julie said. She might have been handling this in her own living room on a beautiful sunny day for all the worry she showed. "Let's play 'I'm Thinking.'"

"What kind of game is that?" Mickey said scornfully.

"It is a game that is lots of fun," Stephen said. Outside the wind was howling. The interior of the barn was gloomy in the diminished light.

"Oh? Have you played 'I'm Thinking' before?" Julie asked, gathering Tonia easily into her lap.

"No," Stephen admitted. "But I'm sure I'll like it." Mickey managed a tentative grin and crept closer to Stephen.

"The way to play the game is this," Julie said. "I will say that I'm thinking of something in the barn that is a certain color or a certain shape. And the rest of you will try to guess what it is. If I said, 'I'm thinking of something in the barn that is long,' for instance, you might guess that it was that long piece of rope hanging on the nail over there. Do you all understand?"

Tonia nodded, looking comfortable in Julie's lap.

"Okay," Julie said over the next roll of thunder, "I'm thinking of something in the barn that is soft."

"The hay!" Mickey exclaimed. "It's soft to sit on!"

"Right," Julie said. "Now you get to think of the next one."

Mickey paused for a moment. "I'm thinking of something in the barn that is a rectangle."

"The bucket!" Tonia shouted.

"No, dummy, a bucket isn't a rectangle."

"The hay!"

Mickey laughed delightedly. "You are so silly, Tonia. The hay is *not* a rectangle!"

Julie's eyes met Stephen's over Tonia's small curly head. He had always known she would be good with children. He was pleased to see that she actually was.

"The door!" Tonia screamed. "The door is a rectangle."

"Good, Tonia. Now you do the 'I'm thinking.'" Mickey settled back, unself-consciously curving himself into Stephen's arms.

The game went on, and the storm raged around the barn. Finally it seemed to lessen, the rain subsiding until it was only a shower. The sound of it on the roof faded from a drumroll to a drone. The air was dank and humid. The four of them were lulled into a sense of safety.

Then Stephen noticed that the light in the barn had turned a peculiar shade of yellow. Startled, he glanced outside the barn.

The black clouds that had been churning so violently in the distance when he left the meadow were now rolling directly overhead, and they seemed to be at a greater height and of a different and more threatening character than the glowering clouds from which the rain had fallen. He stiffened in alarm. Simultaneously he heard the roar.

Stephen jumped to his feet and ran to the barn doorway. Across the pasture he saw a funnel shape dip out of the clouds. It was greenish-yellow around the edges. The hair on the back of his neck rose in prickles.

Julie saw the tornado, too. For a moment they were frozen, unable to move. The gyrating funnel reeled toward them with frightening speed.

"Quickly, over here!" Julie shouted as the din of the tornado filled their ears. It sounded exactly like a freight train.

Stephen couldn't think. Julie shoved him toward the corner so hard that he almost fell. She grabbed Tonia and yanked Mickey by the hand. Julie pushed them all into a pile of hay in the corner of the barn and threw herself on top of the children. Stephen struggled to reach Julie, wanting to protect her.

The tornado hit with the force of a bomb. First Stephen heard a high-pitched whine, and then the wind hurled the bucket against the far wall with a clatter. Hay whirled in the air, dust choked them. Stephen's ears popped, and he couldn't breathe. All at once, the building fell in on them. It seemed like the end of the world.

Then, suddenly, the worst was over. Rain pelted them, stinging their skin, and it seemed eerily quiet. Stephen felt as though he were about to drown in the sound of his own breathing.

When he was sure it was over, Stephen struggled to his feet, trying to make sense of what had happened. Stunned, he saw that the barn was a mass of rubble.

"Juliana," he gasped. The corner of the barn where they had taken shelter was no longer there. Around them lay huge timbers, any one of which, if it had fallen an inch or two closer, would have crushed all of them as they huddled together. Stephen was frantic at the thought that someone might be hurt. He couldn't tell if anyone was hurt—there was too much debris everywhere. He dropped to his knees, totally disoriented.

He knew he had to do something, so he tugged aside a broken piece of wood, and miraculously, Julie sat up. She was coughing.

"Dear God," she choked out, "the children."

Stephen tossed a small uprooted shrub out of the way. Rain glistened on his face.

Then Tonia wailed. Julie pulled the child out of the debris and clasped her to her breast. Beneath Tonia, Mickey struggled to get up.

"Julie! Julie!" Mickey, regaining his voice, began to sob.

"It's all right," Julie said, sitting in the rain, tears streaming down her face. "We're all here." Stephen knelt and put his arms around them, his heart beating madly in his chest. He could not believe their incredible luck.

Someone came running from the direction of the house. It was Albert, white-faced and shaken.

"Were you all together? Is everyone all right?"

Stephen swallowed and nodded. Linda, panicky about her children, raced up. Michael was there, too.

"Inside!" Albert shouted. "We must get inside!"

Michael swept Mickey into his arms, and Linda took Tonia.

"Where? The house or the trailer?" Stephen pulled Julie to her feet. Her ponytail clung in wet streamers to the back of her neck, and she was soaking wet and shivering violently.

"The tornado went in the other direction. We were all in the house, and it didn't touch us. Come on!"

Michael cried, leading the way. Stephen grabbed Julie and supported her as they ran toward the house.

Once inside the door, Julie might have collapsed if Stephen had not held her up. Then competent Carol took over, checking them carefully for broken bones and calming the children. Eva brought blankets while Nonna brewed tea.

"I don't know where it came from," Stephen said to Albert. "One minute it was not there, and the next minute it was. I have never seen anything like it before."

"A thunderstorm can create such a tornado," Albert said, "but I've never seen one up close. It destroyed the barn, but I don't think anything else was harmed, except maybe a few trees. The tornado tore through the pasture and then disappeared. I watched the whole thing from the living room window."

Someone went to call the sheriff's department to report the tornado in case there were other families who lived in the storm's path who might need help.

"We were so lucky," Paul kept repeating. "I don't mind losing the barn. We were going to tear it down eventually. But if any of you had been hurt..." He looked grave.

The sheriff's department reported that the tornado had dissipated before it reached the property of two other families a mile away.

"As tornadoes go, it was a small one," Albert said.

"If you are the one caught in it, no tornado is small," said Paul, who was still shaken from the experience of watching the funnel cloud totally demolish his barn in a matter of seconds.

Amid the general hubbub following the crisis, Stephen approached Julie, who was sitting in a living room chair wrapped in a blanket. She looked worn out, pale and exhausted, but otherwise she seemed fine. He sat down beside her and picked up her hand. He sat caressing it for a time before he spoke.

"You were wonderful in the crisis, Juliana. Wonderful."

She shook her head, prepared to argue.

"No," he said, putting a finger over her lips. "I was there, remember? When I couldn't think, you knew what to do. You protected the children with your own body. I will never forget how you did that, Juliana."

"It was nothing. Anyone would have done the same." Her voice was quiet.

"No, because other people might lose their heads in such a situation. I almost did. When I saw that big funnel and realized what it was, I couldn't move. You were very brave, Juliana."

Her eyes were huge and dark. He knew he couldn't have borne it if anything had happened to this woman. At the thought of what might have happened, his throat swelled and closed. Juliana, crushed beneath a beam. Juliana, cut and bleeding. No, he could not bear it if anything happened to her.

"I was afraid for you, Juliana. Afraid that something had happened to you. And in the moment before I knew that you were all right, I was sick at heart."

"Oh, Stephen," was all she said, but he knew from the look in her eyes that she had felt the same way about him.

And he knew now that whatever it was that kept Julie off the high wire, it wasn't lack of nerve. She had proved that she could function in a crisis. No, it was something else entirely.

He would never give up until he discovered what it was.

THE TORNADO that hit the Andrassy barn was one of many spawned by the storm. One of the tornadoes, a much more destructive one, smashed through a trailer park outside nearby Cornelia and killed three people. A television crew sent to Cornelia from Atlanta heard about the tornado at the Andrassy place and stopped by to talk to Paul.

"I'm not the one who was in the tornado," Paul told them. "If you want to know what it was really like, you need to talk to Stephen Andrassy."

"Stephen Andrassy," the reporter said, gazing at the pile of rubble that had once been the barn. "Where have I heard of him before?"

"He was a top performer with the Big Apple Circus in New York," Paul prompted. "He also worked at the Moscow Circus."

"Moscow, *Russia*?" asked the reporter incredulously.

"You remember," one of the cameramen said. "The story was on all the networks last January. He's the one who defected from the Soviet Union."

"Oh, *that* Stephen Andrassy," the reporter said. "You mean he's here? At your place?"

"He and the rest of the Andrassy performing troupe are rehearsing here," said Paul, who firmly believed that if life hands you a lemon, you should make lemonade. "They're taking their act on the high wire soon."

"Say," the reporter said, the light dawning. "Aren't you all from the same family? The family that fell at the Superdome a few years back?"

"We are," Paul replied.

"I want to talk to this Stephen Andrassy. Maybe we can do a feature for our noon news program."

"I think Stephen would like that very much," said Paul, who considered the loss of a barn insignificant compared to the publicity its loss could generate for the Amazing Andrassys.

"STEPHEN, YOU TALK TO THEM. I don't want to." Julie flicked a switch in her eyes and the light went out of them; Stephen recognized this particular expression as one she adopted when she was intent on being obstinate.

"Juliana, you were the one who saved the children. You should be part of the feature they're doing."

"It's not a feature about surviving the tornado. You know very well that the TV station is going to concentrate on the story of the Amazing Andrassys returning to the high wire."

"But you belong in such a story," Stephen said, wondering why he was bothering to argue. It was a feature about the family returning to the wire, but the reporter wanted to show the viewers how their return to the wire was a family enterprise.

"No, Stephen," Julie said. "Leave me out of it."

"Ah, Juliana," Stephen sighed in exasperation. He hurried off to tell the TV crew that Julie would not participate in the film, and Julie watched him walk away.

It did seem strange, now that the Amazing Andrassys were getting closer to their debut on the wire. She had been brought up to be a part of the act, and now she was not. It was a peculiar feeling, this being left out of something that everyone else was so enthusiastic about.

But, she thought grimly, she would just have to get used to it, because that was the way things had to be.

THE ANDRASSYS gave thanks for the sparing of their family members' lives at a big dinner the next night. Nonna cooked a huge pot of her famous goulash, and Julie baked a birthday cake. It was also Nonna's seventy-seventh birthday celebration.

"Make a wish, make a wish," Tonia cried, none the worse for her experience with the tornado.

"Oh, I don't know what to wish for," Nonna said, smiling broadly. "My wish that my family could be together again has come true."

"Wish that the Amazing Andrassys will make a successful comeback," Eva suggested.

"Yes, I will wish for that," Nonna said. "But Mickey must blow out the candles for me."

Mickey blew out every candle, and the Andrassys cheered.

"When will the Amazing Andrassys perform for the first time in public?" Sam asked.

"It will be in September at a Shriners' convention," Stephen said. "I am in the process of getting a contract with a promoter now."

"In September! So soon!" Susan exclaimed. "Will we be ready?"

"We will be ready. Of course, I would feel better if we had not lost the barn in the tornado. With the barn we were assured of a place to practice even if the weather is bad. There are often afternoon thunderstorms here in the summer, Paul tells me. But if we cannot practice so late in the afternoon, we will have to start practicing earlier in the morning. It is the best time to practice, anyway."

"It's okay if I practice with them, isn't it, Mom?" Sam asked anxiously. He had been mightily impressed that the performing troupe was going to be on television.

Carol and Paul exchanged a meaningful look.

"It will be all right, I guess," Carol said quietly. "As long as Stephen is there to supervise."

Julie stood up abruptly from the table. She gathered several plates and took them into the kitchen, where she set them on the counter and stood in the middle of the floor, unwilling to go back into the dining room. She hated to see Sam caught up in this Andrassy madness to get back on the high wire.

"Julie—" It was Carol.

"I'm all right. Don't mind me." The words came out clipped and short. For the lack of anything better to do, she grabbed the coffeepot, carried it into the dining room and moved around the table, pouring everyone more coffee.

"Gee, Nonna, I wish you didn't have to leave so soon. We're going to be here all summer." Tonia hugged her great-grandmother's arm.

"I wish I didn't have to leave, too," Nonna said. "But Julie has to be back at work on Monday."

At that moment Stephen's eyes locked with Julie's, and Julie's hand began to tremble so much that she couldn't pour. She fled into the kitchen, even though Paul's cup could have used a refill.

"I do wish you two could stay a bit longer," Paul said to Julie when she slid back into her seat at the table. "Carol's younger son, Eric, is coming home from camp on Sunday. He's a great kid, and I'd like you and Nonna to see him.''

''Well, we'll be gone by then,'' Julie said, cutting into her slice of birthday cake. She knew Stephen was looking at her, his expression serious. The cake turned to dust in her mouth.

Why didn't he look somewhere else? Why did he have to stare? Someone would notice; someone would see. She was smothering in a tangle of emotions.

She heard them chattering around her, all the Andrassys, but she didn't know what they said. She saw them, but only peripherally. For Julie, Stephen was the only person at the table. They faced each other across the wide table spotted with gravy and dotted with crumbs, and the other Andrassys might as well have not been there at all.

In a daze she fancied that she could read his thoughts. *Don't go,* he was crying out to her. *Stay.* His eyes pleaded with her, and she couldn't avoid them.

Quickly she stood and pushed her chair back with a clatter.

''I—I think I'll go and lie down for a while,'' she stammered to no one in particular. ''I think my experience with the tornado yesterday affected me more than I thought.''

The family conversation dimmed, like the volume turned down on a radio, and then it swelled again as she ran up the stairs. Julie heard her name uttered a couple of times, but she couldn't tell who spoke it. Then she was in the room she shared with Susan and Eva, and she was alone. She shut the door and locked it before throwing herself across the bed.

He was in love with her. She hadn't had much experience with men being in love with her, but even her limited experience had prepared her to recognize the intense emotion shining from Stephen's blue eyes. He was in love with her. What should she do about it?

What she should do about it depended on how she felt about him. She turned over on her back and stared up at the light fixture on the ceiling. How *did* she feel about Stephen Martinovic-Andrassy?

She felt close to him. She had discovered that she could talk to him about serious personal concerns, and he was understanding, kind, and dealt with her worries in a straightforward, common-sense sort of way. And, after the other night in her car, she knew that she was incredibly aroused by him.

"Julie? It's Eva. Are you all right?" Her cousin rattled the doorknob.

"I'm okay," Julie said. She went and unlocked the door. "You can come in if you want."

"We're all going for a walk down to the barn. Or at least to where the barn used to be. We want to take a look at it before Paul's workmen clear away the rubble tomorrow. Do you want to come along with us?"

Julie shook her head. "No. I—I have a headache."

"You're not sick? Do you want me to get Carol?"

"No, please don't. I'll take an aspirin and rest." Julie attempted a reassuring smile.

"Well, okay. I thought you were all right, but Stephen insisted that I come up and make sure you weren't gasping your last. I'll reassure him, don't worry." Eva whirled around and ran downstairs.

"Stephen," Julie murmured thoughtfully, closing the door. Again, proof that he cared about her, that he loved her. She knew she had not mistaken the passionate yearning in his eyes, the sense of deep attraction. Suddenly her spirits soared and she felt euphoric. He loved her! Shouldn't that be cause for happiness?

Her mood fizzled as quickly as it had developed. She could never love a man who walked the high wire for a living.

No matter how good he was at it, no matter how careful, the possibility always existed that Stephen would die of his terrible obsession. All the reassurances in the world didn't matter, all the safety precautions didn't matter, because in the end, what counted was that Stephen walked on a cable high above the ground, and in a split second he could falter, hang for a moment in midair and fall. Death did not walk the high wire; it lurked below. And it didn't go away. It was always there, lying in wait for those who dared to defy it.

She could never let herself love Stephen Andrassy.

She shook with a sudden chill. Something tightened around her heart, an icy band of pain, and she knew that she had to accept the truth: She could never love this man.

There was no need ever to confront the situation with Stephen. She could maneuver and manipulate their meetings so that they were never alone, so that they never talked privately. She would never give him the chance to speak of love.

It wouldn't be so hard, this avoiding him. After all, she and Nonna would be leaving soon. They would be driving back to Florida in two days.

TRY AS HE MIGHT, Stephen couldn't get Julie alone. She had slept late for the past two mornings, which was unusual for her. He and the others had already gone to the meadow by the time she got up. At lunchtime on Thursday she simply wasn't there. When he had commented casually on her absence, Susan had said something about Julie's having errands to run in town.

He planned to ask Julie to go for a walk alone with him after dinner, but she and Eva went off to the movies without asking anyone else to join them. And afterward, Julie and Eva had retired early. Stephen had paced up and down the floor of the small sewing room where he slept, knowing that time was short.

This day, Friday, Julie had gone down to Michael's trailer to eat lunch with Linda and the children. In the evening, she had said she had to pack. She went to the room she shared with Susan and Eva at seven-thirty, and she hadn't come out again.

She was avoiding him. He realized that now. What had he done? Had he said the wrong thing? He was desperate to speak with her, to establish their special kind of closeness again, if only for an hour. She was going back to Florida the next day. He had no idea when he would see her again.

The phone rang downstairs. Stephen sat on the couch that was his bed and ignored it. There was no upstairs extension.

"Julie!" Carol called up the stairwell. "Telephone for you! It sounds like long-distance."

Julie's door flew open, and suddenly Stephen felt a glimmer of hope. If she came out of her room, he might be able to catch her for a brief moment. It wouldn't be enough time to tell her all that was in his heart, but it would be a beginning.

Julie flew downstairs, her hair, loose for once, curling around her shoulder.

"I've got it!" Julie called from the living room to the kitchen. Stephen stood and went to the banister, leaning over to watch. Her dark eyes seemed burnished with gold in the light from the small lamp on the table at the foot of the stairs.

"Oh, no," Julie was saying, her voice full of anxiety. "Oh, how awful." After a pause she said in bleak resignation, "Well, how long?"

Stephen listened more closely. It was obvious from the expression on Julie's face that this was bad news. Nonna appeared in the doorway to the dining room, a concerned expression on her face.

Julie replaced the telephone receiver on its hook. "It's Molly," she said dully, "my best student. She's broken her leg."

"The little gymnast? The one who is so good?" Slowly Nonna made her way to Julie and circled her waist with one arm. "Julie, I am sorry."

"She was thrown from a horse. She'll be in a cast for at least three months."

"Oh, no."

"And I had such high hopes for her next meet. Of course, Molly's devastated, too."

Stephen slowly descended the stairs, ready to offer his sympathy. He knew that Julie set great store by this particular student.

"But—but, Julie! Think what this means!" Nonna's face was alight with happiness.

Julie shook her head. "It means I don't have a student to teach. I was planning to devote all my time to Molly this summer while the work load is light. Most of our gymnastics students take the summer months off for camp and summer vacations with their families."

"Yes, and that is what we will do, also!" Nonna clapped her hands together like a young girl. "Don't you see, Julie? This means that we do not have to leave tomorrow! We can spend the whole summer right here at the farm!"

Chapter Seven

Julie managed to stay out of Stephen's way for most of the next week. It wasn't hard, with so many Andrassys around. Eric, Carol's fourteen-year-old son, arrived home from camp, which added to the confusion. With something going on all the time that the cousins weren't practicing on the wire, there was no opportunity for Stephen to catch Julie alone.

Stephen was busy with his own concerns. The phone rang constantly, and it was often for him. The television feature film that had been shown on the Atlanta station early in the week generated a lot of interest in the act. Stephen was constantly fielding questions about when they would perform, where they would perform, and whether it was true that they would attempt the famous Andrassy pyramid?

The promoter who was planning the Amazing Andrassys' comeback performance called often, and Julie overheard Stephen negotiating the contract. She heard the others talking about his hardheadedness in hammering out a good deal for the act. Stephen was well aware of the act's marketability. This somehow surprised Julie. She knew that Stephen was a star performer; he could not have performed with the Moscow Circus if he hadn't been. But she hadn't expected him to be a good businessman as well.

Nonna, after her insistence on staying at the farm, was in her element. She taught little Tonia to sew, and all the Andrassys were reluctant recipients of calico bags loosely sewn together with Tonia's giant stitches. Nonna even found an old bag of Eric's marbles, and coached by Eric, she could be found kneeling with her great-grandson at the edge of a circle inscribed in the dust, tossing around words like "aggy" and "immy." In the evenings Nonna huddled with Sam and Eric at the dining room table, totally in character as an elf in their ongoing game of Dungeons and Dragons. Oh, yes, no doubt about it—Nonna was having a wonderful time.

But Julie wasn't. Time hung heavy on her hands. She started one of Eva's thick paperback novels, but couldn't concentrate on it for very long at one time. She helped Carol with the cooking and laundry for this huge family, though she had to admit to herself that, with Nonna's help, Carol was capable of doing all of it without Julie's assistance. She visited with Linda, Michael's cute redheaded wife, whom she had never really gotten to know before, but twenty minutes of discussion about what color socks to buy Tonia and what to do about Mickey's teasing of his sister bored Julie to distraction.

Plus, Julie was having a hard time sleeping at night. Susan and Eva always dropped off right away, exhausted from their hours of practice. Julie would lie on her bed staring into the dark, restless and wide-awake. She was used to vigorous physical activity day after day at the gym. To lead a relatively inactive life went against her grain. Worst of all, she was bound to get out of shape if she didn't get some sort of exercise during the next couple of months.

One night as she was lying wide-awake in her bed, Julie decided to start an exercise program the very next day. That way she could keep in shape; also, maybe she'd be able to sleep better at night if she exercised.

As she lay there, she heard the floorboards creak down at the end of the hall. She knew from experience that the sound came from the sewing room where Stephen slept—or did not sleep, which seemed to be the case at the moment. She shifted over on her side, listening to Eva's soft breathing in the next bed. If only she could stop thinking about Stephen!

Her emotions simmered beneath her cool demeanor. Thoughts of Stephen sprang from a seemingly inexhaustible wellspring, overwhelming her at the oddest times. It didn't take much to start the images flowing, images of Stephen with his thoughtful blue eyes, his straight corn-silk hair, his compact and lean physique, the murmur of his voice, which she could call to mind with no effort at all. The rich rumble of his laughter, the touch of his hand on her shoulder, the satiny smoothness of his lips. Oh, it all stayed with her, seldom far from her consciousness. She had never been so obsessed with a man before.

She tossed, burning, beneath the cool white sheets. Yes, an exercise program was a very good idea. She'd begin by running a couple of miles the very next morning.

JULIE WAS UP AT DAWN. She pulled on her running shorts and a sleeveless shirt, jostling Eva's bed as she bent over to tie the shoelaces of her running shoes.

"Wha?" Eva mumbled as she opened one eye to the sight of a gray dawn and Julie feverishly bundling her unruly hair into a knot at the back of her head.

"Go back to sleep," Julie whispered before creeping down the dim hall to the bathroom to brush her teeth.

The air was chilly, but Julie knew that by the time she finished running, the sun would have warmed things up considerably. At the moment, the sun was a mere orange glow behind the stand of trees on the other side of the house. She bent and pulled her socks over her calves, then set off at a brisk walk to warm up. By the time Julie reached the driveway, she had hit her stride. She plowed through curling remnants of the morning mist, her spirits lifting. She wondered why she hadn't thought of this long ago.

She focused totally on her stride, making her legs reach out as far as they could. She ran lightly, easily, feeling the fresh air sweep the cobwebs out of her brain. She would run all the way to the road, then continue along it to the Andrassy Acres subdivision, circling until she came to the meadow where the practice wires were set up. She could get back to the house just in time for breakfast.

One reason she loved to run was that she didn't have to think of anything else. Her mind was lulled into a sort of peace by the rhythmic *slap-slap* of her feet on pavement, and her body became engrossed in its task. She jogged past the mailbox that said "Andrassy" and turned west toward the subdivision.

A car whooshed by, and then another. By the time she reached Andrassy Acres, she was feeling pleasantly tired, but she was still running at peak efficiency. She ran past the sites of two new houses in different stages of construction and on to the end of the road where there was a gate leading to the meadow. Remembering her broken fingernail, she didn't hassle with the latch. Instead, she climbed agilely over the fence and dropped to the grass on the other side.

She ran along the old cow path and rounded a stand of trees. In the distance she saw the high wire. She was surprised to see that someone was on it.

She ran on, aware of the beating of her heart. Then she slowed to a stop. She stood, her chest heaving, and tucked errant wisps of hair behind her ears. There was no mistaking the figure on the high wire. It was Stephen.

Why was he out here so early in the morning? She walked several steps, hands on her hips, breathing heavily. As she drew closer, she saw that Stephen was alone.

She moved slowly toward him, taking no pains to conceal her presence. Even if she had not wished to be seen, it wouldn't have been necessary to hide. Stephen was totally engrossed in what he was doing. He was aware of nothing and no one.

He was silhouetted against the opalescent sky of sunrise, and his stance was majestic, magnificent. He seemed illumined with light from within. His hair, pale and fine, blew gently in the slight breeze; he stood immobile. At the same time he managed to look both determined and transfixed by whatever drove him to walk the wire. He was beautiful.

Mesmerized, she watched as Stephen knelt on the cable, then, with exquisite grace, lay down so that one foot swung beneath it. He remained like that, totally at ease as he rested and contemplated the transformation of sky from gray to pink to blue.

If she moved forward now, he might see that she had been watching. Or was his concentration so deep that he still saw nothing? Julie felt as though she had caught Stephen in the middle of something very private. She wished she had left the meadow as soon as she'd realized that it was he on the wire.

One thing for sure—she didn't want him to see her now. Feeling shamefully like a voyeur, she tiptoed forward and crouched in a nest of tall grass. The grass was damp, and the dew penetrated her shorts. She didn't care; she couldn't take her eyes off Stephen.

After a time—Julie didn't know how long—Stephen rose from the wire as gracefully as he had stretched himself upon it. He stood, face to the sky, and then, slowly and surely, slid one foot forward, then the other. Every muscle was in control, every molecule of his being was concentrated on the cable.

Alone he dared the sky; alone he touched the stars. Clearly he savored his solitude. And Julie, hiding in her nest of grass, was shaken to her core by the rightness of it all. Stephen had spoken to her of the peace of giving himself to the wire completely and centering down until he felt at one with the air. Stephen's perfection and mastery of his art moved Julie quite unexpectedly. She let out a shaky breath as she realized that Stephen Andrassy didn't so much control the wire as he made it a part of himself. As much as Julie hated the high wire, she couldn't deny, after watching Stephen, that of all the places in the universe, it was the right place for him.

She dared not let him see her here. If he did, he would know what she thought. He would know that his performance had stirred her in a strange and wondrous way. And she didn't want him to know that she had finally and illogically admitted to herself that walking the wire was what Stephen was meant to do with his life. She could hardly believe that her thinking had changed so radically.

Carefully she stood; carefully she made her way back to the trees at the edge of the meadow. She wouldn't cut through the meadow, after all; she would go back to the house through the subdivision, the way she had come.

Her last view of Stephen before she rounded the bend in the path was of him crossing the wire, surefooted and erect, his arms joyfully outstretched toward the rising sun.

"STEPHEN! STEPHEN!" Eric called to the troupe of wire walkers as they made their way up from the meadow for lunch. "Telephone!"

Stephen broke into a run. "Thanks, Eric," he said, clapping the boy on the back as he reached the front porch. He hurried inside, slamming the screen door behind him.

Julie arranged tuna sandwiches on a plate and shot Stephen a sidelong look as he rapped out words into the kitchen telephone.

"Yes? Yes, I can see you today." There was a pent-up excitement in Stephen's tone, and she wondered who the caller was. She wondered even more when Stephen gave him the directions from the town of Peaceable Kingdom to the farm.

"I am expecting a guest tonight," Stephen announced as they ate lunch.

"Who?" asked Eva, not as unwilling to show her curiosity as Julie was.

"Oh, a man from Atlanta. Please pass the carrot sticks, will you, Sam?"

It was not lost on Julie that they still didn't know the identity of Stephen's visitor, and Stephen didn't seem inclined to enlighten them. Nothing more was said about it until a man wearing sunglasses and a gray business suit drove up in a car with an Avis Rental sticker on the windshield. Stephen hurried out to meet him, and the two of them closeted themselves in the sewing room that served as Stephen's bedroom and office. It was two hours before they came out.

Julie, who was sitting on the front porch sharing conversation and a peach with Paul, noticed that Stephen seemed aquiver with excitement as he walked his guest to his car. There was only one thing that could engender such enthusiasm in Stephen—something to do with walking the wire.

"What was that all about?" Paul asked, tossing the peach pit over the porch railing as Stephen mounted the steps.

"It is—" Stephen stopped when he saw the expression of dread on Julie's face. It was as though she had guessed, as though she knew. But no one knew; he had just made his final decision a few minutes ago. He cleared his throat. He would have to handle this carefully, for Julie's sake.

"Come inside," he said. "I have an announcement to make."

Silently Julie and Paul followed him into the house. The family gathered around them in the living room. Carol switched on a lamp.

"It is settled," Stephen said. "And you shall all be the first to know. In order to get publicity for the return of the Amazing Andrassys to the high wire, I have just signed a contract to appear on the television show *Thrills!*"

"You, Stephen? You alone?" Susan asked anxiously.

"Yes. Me alone."

"But that's one of the hit shows of the summer season! They show famous daredevil acts, like the guy who jumps a bunch of school buses on his motorcycle," Eric said.

"How will you fit into that?" Michael asked in a puzzled tone. "The Amazing Andrassys aren't exactly daredevils. We're performers!"

"We are performers, yes. But we can also be daredevils at times, depending on where we perform."

"And where are you going to perform?" Julie whispered, fear stabbing into her heart.

Stephen looked deep into her eyes. His look begged for understanding. In that one blank startling second, she knew.

"I," he said slowly and with a sense of drama, "I am going to walk a cable across the Tallulah Gorge."

It was completely quiet. Then the room erupted with questions, with astonished exclamations. Everyone talked at once, crowding around Stephen. Julie stumbled blindly toward the front door. No one would miss her now; no one would see her leave.

No one, that is, except Stephen himself. His eyes followed her as she slowly let herself out, her movements wooden and her eyes dull.

JULIE GOT INTO HER CAR and drove, to keep herself
from thinking—thinking of the wild and awesome
Tallulah Gorge, and of Stephen suspended above it.

Her Ford swallowed up the miles to town until,
ahead of her, she saw the stoplight in Peaceable Kingdom. She slowed down, intending to drive on. But as
she sat at the red light, she realized that beyond the
town lay only a dark and lonely road. If she didn't do
something to distract herself, she'd think about Stephen crossing the Gorge, and she didn't want to do
that. Abruptly she turned the corner and swung her
car into a diagonal parking place not far from the
Peaceable Kingdom Cinema.

It was a Friday night, and the locals had turned out
in force to cruise the town. Cars circled the courthouse square, then peeled off at the stoplight. Kids
leaned out of car windows, yelling to their friends on
the sidewalk. A carnival atmosphere prevailed, and
that was all to the good for Julie's purposes. She got
out of her car and locked the door.

Without really thinking about it, she found herself
standing in line waiting to buy a ticket to the movie.
There were twin theaters inside; she and Eva had already seen the science fiction feature playing in Cinema 1. Okay, she'd go to Cinema 2, then. It didn't
matter where she went, just so long as there was
something to fill her field of vision, anything other
than the mental picture of Stephen crossing Tallulah
Gorge.

STEPHEN SAW JULIE standing in line in front of the
Cinema and, surprised, braked the car he had bor-
rowed from Paul. He was glad he had found her in so

ordinary a place. He'd had no idea where she'd intended to go.

She was feeling this—he could tell. Julie looked somehow smaller and dimmer than she was supposed to look. Her skin was sallow in the wash of bright lights from the theater marquee. His heart went out to her.

He joined her in line, as though he were supposed to have been there all the time. The people behind her glared at him for breaking in. He hoped they'd think he'd been parking their car, that he was Julie's date—or husband.

She looked up at him, squinting a little.

"Which movie are you going to see?" he asked her.

She shrugged. "Not the science fiction one. The other one."

He paid for the tickets and she stood aside, unprotesting. He hadn't expected her to be so passive, somehow. He followed her inside.

An overzealous boy wearing a white paper cap stood behind the popcorn machine, keeping up a steady chatter as the moviegoers entered the theater.

"How about some popcorn, miss? Fresh-made popcorn, get it right here. Sure, here's a jumbo-size box. Have a cold drink to go with it? Step to the right, the girl at the end of the counter will help you. Lots of fresh, buttered popcorn! How about it, sir? Popcorn for you?"

Stephen was startled when he realized that the boy was talking to him.

"Er, yes," he said, inserting his hand into the pocket of his jeans and pulling out some change. The boy handed him a red-and-white striped cardboard box.

"And how about some for your lady?" he said.

"My la—? Oh, of course. Juliana? Would you care for popcorn?"

Julie shook her head, her eyebrows winging upward and managing to make her look like a startled fawn. Without thinking Stephen curved his free arm around her shoulders. It seemed like the natural thing to do, but he was chastened when Julie shook his arm off and strode ahead of him into the darkened theater.

She sat down in the middle of the left-hand section about midway down the aisle. He sat down beside her. She kept her eyes steadfastly fastened on the screen as the movie credits skated past.

They put their elbows on their shared armrest at exactly the same time. For a moment, their arms jostled for the space. She felt the slight stiffening of his muscles. Then Stephen removed his arm. So did she. The armrest seemed to grow between them, a visible barrier.

Julie felt herself shrink, as though to inhabit less space and to breathe less air. If she could have, she would have disappeared altogether, rather than sit here beside Stephen, unable to let herself acknowledge that they were together while they were feeling so very far apart. She felt conscious of every move he made, whether it was to dig in the popcorn box for a handful of popcorn or to push his seat into a more comfortable position. She was aware of the pores on the back of his hand and of the brightness of his pale hair in the darkened theater. She knew when he moved his foot and when he flicked a popcorn kernel off his knee. Oh, she was aware of him all right, and she was miserable about it.

The movie had no discernible plot as far as Julie could tell, and the only character with any continuity seemed to be a souped-up red Camaro. But the movie served its purpose. The chase scenes and loud twangy music distracted her from the things she didn't want to think about. Even if Stephen had wanted to talk to her, he wouldn't have been able to. For those things she was grateful.

Stephen sat beside her, frowning slightly and seemingly concentrating on the film. Julie stole an occasional glance at him, almost as one would steal a look at something forbidden. When this thought occurred to her, she nearly laughed, despite the sadness in her heart. Something forbidden. Well, he was that, all right—forever forbidden to her because of what he did for a living.

Blinking back tears, she forced herself to watch the mayhem on the screen. She had almost admitted to herself that she loved Stephen. And that, of course, would never do.

HE FOLLOWED HER OUT of the movie theater. She didn't speak; apparently, she didn't intend to.

"Juliana, please don't go. Not yet."

She shot him a look over her shoulder and continued walking. He caught up with her and grabbed her arm. A policeman cruising past in a patrol car slowed down, hanging an arm out the car window and watching them to see what happened next.

"Little lady, is the man bothering you?"

Julie started. "No, officer, everything is fine."

Shaken, Stephen removed his hand from Julie's arm, and when the policeman saw that everything was apparently all right, he speeded up and disappeared on the other side of the courthouse. Stephen cringed inside. To think that anyone would think he would hurt Julie!

But the exchange with the policeman had apparently amused her. She visibly loosened up, and her face stopped looking so pinched and drawn.

Stephen kept his voice low so that passersby wouldn't hear. "Juliana, I want to tell you about the Tallulah Gorge," he began.

"I know about it. You took me there, remember?" Her voice sounded metallic, like a plucked string on a steel guitar.

"Of course I remember. It was one of the most pleasant days I have ever had."

In fleeing the movie theater, Julie had, in her disorientation, turned the wrong way. She stopped walking. "My car is back there," she said. She wheeled and began to walk in the other direction. He pivoted accordingly and kept up with her rapid pace.

"You took me to Tallulah Gorge so you could check it out for your walk, didn't you? Didn't you?" Her dark eyes glittered up at him accusingly.

"That was one reason I went there," he admitted. "The other reason was to spend time with you."

"All the time we were there, you were figuring out where to fasten the guy lines, how to rig your cable. Right?"

"It was part of it."

"*Why*, Stephen? Why must you walk the Gorge?"

"I *want* to do it. It is a challenge to my experience and my art. And it is valuable publicity for the act, Juliana. When people know that Stephen Andrassy walked the Tallulah Gorge, they will be eager to pay money to see the Amazing Andrassys on the high wire again.''

"Is that all you ever think about?" Julie exploded. "The *act*?"

Stephen waited until a rowdy group of young people passed, laughing and talking on their way to the Pizza Hut for a snack after the movie.

"No, Juliana. It is not all I think about. I think about you quite often. About the way you feel about us going on the high wire. And other things. You are my friend. Or at least I thought you were."

Julie felt deflated. "I am your friend," she said heavily.

"Even though I walk the high wire?" he asked softly.

"In spite of it," she whispered. "In spite of it."

"I tell you, Juliana, I need your friendship and support for what I am about to do. Negative thoughts I do not need. They are dangerous. They infect everyone and everything they come into contact with. Do not persist in thinking negative thoughts. Please."

They had reached her car now. Julie raised her eyes to his. He was right. If she cared at all about him, she wouldn't put additional handicaps in his path. The task he had set for himself was difficult enough as it was.

"Can we go in the Pizza Hut and get a pizza?" he said. "Can we talk the way we used to? I have missed talking with you lately, Juliana."

It was the way he said her name, so unlike the way anyone else ever pronounced it, that won her over.

"All right," she said. She turned and walked ahead of him into the restaurant, part of a group they'd seen at the movie. Quietly they detached themselves from the others and found a booth for two.

Over their pizza Stephen conceded, "I know there are people who will say I'm crazy for walking the Gorge. But those kinds of people I shut out of my mind. I don't let them, or their dire predictions, in. And I don't want to shut you out, Juliana. I want your good wishes."

"You have those," she said, meaning it.

"And your confidence in me."

She thought for a moment, remembering Stephen's mastery of the cable on that morning when she had secretly watched him greeting the sunrise.

"I have confidence in you," she said slowly and with a certain amount of surprise at herself.

Stephen grinned a radiant grin. "Then that is all I want."

"I would never try to undermine you, Stephen. You must know that." She spoke earnestly, wondering how all her barriers seemed to fall away when she and Stephen were face to face, talking.

He swallowed a piece of pizza and washed it down with beer. "I know. How long will it be until you can give me your active enthusiasm?"

Julie shuddered. "I don't know. That's a lot to ask."

"Juliana, *why* can't you forget what happened in the Superdome so long ago? The others have forgotten!" His eyes, an electric blue, challenged her.

"Because I am not the others!" she gritted through clenched teeth. "It was different for me!"

"Because you were not on the wire that night? Is that why?"

She paled. "I—I—"

"You were not on the wire and you feel guilty, don't you? Because you weren't up there with the others."

"Stop it," she begged. "Stop. You don't know what happened; you don't know anything about it. You weren't there!"

"But the others were, Juliana. Shall I talk to them about it?"

"No," she whispered, feeling faint. "Please don't. You wouldn't, would you?"

His heart melted at the sight of her, looking so hurt, so guilty.

"I would never do anything to hurt you," he said solemnly. "We are friends."

"Friends," she repeated dully. *Friends,* she thought. *And there's one other little detail that neither of us has mentioned. We also love each other.* It was the first time she had admitted to herself that she loved him. The thought made her miserable, because loving Stephen Andrassy promised nothing but a life of heart-wrenching sadness. What was the matter with her? Why had she let love happen to her?

"Check, please," Stephen said to the waitress. As they waited for it, he leaned across the table. He misunderstood her obvious wretchedness for something else.

"If you ever want to talk about that night in New Orleans, Juliana, I will be happy to listen. It seems to me that you have not talked of it enough."

"I haven't ever talked about it," she said unhappily. "To anyone." Her eyes, dark-fringed and tense, met his over the flickering candle.

"If you ever want to," he repeated, "remember that I am your friend."

Much more than my friend, she thought. But she said, "I'll remember," and she knew that she would never want to talk about that long-ago night in New Orleans. Not to anyone.

Chapter Eight

The others were beginning to notice the strain between Julie and Stephen.

Paul even mentioned it.

"I'm worried about you, Julie," he said one evening when they were outside at the brick barbecue pit overseeing the charcoal broiling of hamburgers for the family dinner.

"Oh?" Julie said, concentrating on turning the meat. "Why is that?"

"You've been so quiet ever since you've been on the farm. That's not the way I remember you, Julie. You were always so bubbly, so full of life."

"You and I haven't spent much time together since the days when we performed on the wire, Paul." She made a great effort to keep her voice even.

"No, that's true." He paused as though considering what he was going to say.

"Julie," he went on, "I know you don't think much of the others' decision to go back on the wire."

"That's right, I don't."

"It's inevitable now. They're going to do it. So, if you've been hoping that something might happen, that they might give up on the idea, you might as well stop thinking it." His voice was quiet but firm.

Julie sighed. "I know. But it's hard for me, being here on the farm with all of them, watching the preparations. If it weren't for Nonna, I wouldn't have come."

"You and Nonna—is she getting to be too much for you?"

Julie glanced up at him, surprised at his perceptiveness.

"She hasn't been well, of course. But she's really dear, and we live together happily. Or at least we did before Stephen came." The last sentence tumbled out before she could stop it, and she immediately regretted her words.

"Do you resent him so much, Julie?" Paul seemed genuinely concerned.

"I—I—" She couldn't answer this. Yes, she resented Stephen. But she also loved him. There was no way to explain this to her cousin. Or even to herself.

"I watched your face the night Stephen told us he was going to walk the Tallulah Gorge. You turned chalk-white. You're really upset about it, aren't you?"

"I've seen the Gorge," she said. "The sandstone walls seem to bend. It makes you lose your perspective. One look down and a person could become dizzy. It's not like walking a wire anywhere else. The Gorge is a place where it would be all too easy to lose your bearings. Stephen shouldn't be allowed to walk it, Paul. It's like going out and asking to be killed!"

"Stephen knows what he's doing. He'll make it. I don't have any doubt about his ability to complete a successful crossing. If I did, I wouldn't have agreed to set up the rigging."

The spatula clattered as Julie dropped it. "*You*, Paul? You're going to do the rigging?"

Paul nodded. "We all are, all the male members of the family—Michael, Albert and me. Stephen will plan his rigging carefully, and he's hired about twenty local fellows to do the work, but he needs people he can trust to oversee the placing of the cavallettis, to work the winches, to check the anchors, because Stephen can't be everywhere at once."

"Dear Lord, am I the only one who thinks this is crazy? Am I the only one who thinks this is wrong?" Shaking her head in disbelief, Julie backed away from the grill and stood with her fists clenched as though to do battle with anyone of a different opinion.

"You're probably not the only one in the world who feels that way, Julie, but it's a sure thing you're the only one of the Andrassys who does!"

"The Andrassys, the Andrassys! Do you know how sick I am of hearing about the Andrassys?" Julie cried, and then she whirled around and ran inside the house.

Paul had always been so calm, so reasonable. He was her oldest cousin, and she had always respected him. Besides Julie, he was the only able Andrassy who had refused to go back on the wire. And even he thought she was wrong to feel the way she did!

After that, her family took on a different character when she was around. Julie was not immune to conversations that hushed when she walked into the room, to references to practice that were glossed over when she was present. Where the Andrassys once might have been uninhibited in talking about their art, they were now subdued, even evasive. Julie knew that a conspiracy to protect her delicate sensibilities was afoot among members of the family, and that Paul had probably instigated it. They were doing it out of love, she knew, but it only made her feel uncomfortable. If only everyone would act more natural around her!

The Fourth of July intervened to provide a release from the tension surrounding them. Carol, who had been worried about the unspoken apprehension in her household, planned a Fourth chock-full of family activities.

Stephen was exuberant about the celebration of his first Fourth of July.

"It is not only my first Fourth of July, but it is my first Fourth of July with the family. I want all of you to help me celebrate not only the independence of the United States, but my independence, too!"

"Oh, we'll celebrate, all right," Sam assured him. "We always do."

"Doesn't the town of Peaceable Kingdom have anything going on for the Fourth?" Julie asked when it appeared that all of the day's events were to take place on the farm.

Carol only laughed. "In this town, there's never a public celebration of the Fourth. Independence Day is a Yankee holiday, Julie."

"But surely they've gotten over the Civil War by this time!" exclaimed Eva, who was shocked.

"When I went to Peaceable Kingdom High School, we still got out of school on Confederate Memorial Day. No, if we want to celebrate Independence Day, we'll have to do it in our own way. Aside from the Fourth of July races at the municipal pool, nothing is happening in town. Anyway, most people will go to Lake Lanier or drive over to the beach for the weekend."

"The beach?"

"Sure. Savannah, Charleston or Myrtle."

"Hey, Stephen," Susan called. "Why don't we all go to the beach for the weekend?"

"No, no one leaves the farm. Because we must practice every day of that weekend but the Fourth itself."

Carol asked Julie to be in charge of entertainment for this special day.

"Entertainment?" Julie asked, looking askance. "What kind of entertainment?"

"Games and things," Carol said airily. "You know."

"I'm in charge of food," Nonna said.

"I'm in charge of fireworks," Sam said.

"You are?" Eric asked. "I thought I was."

"We both are," amended his brother. "We'll drive across the state line to South Carolina and buy the fireworks tomorrow."

EXCITEMENT ABOUT the Fourth of July infected everyone in the family.

"I can hardly wait," Tonia confided to Julie one day when they were shucking ears of corn together on the back porch. "I can hardly wait for the Fourth of July."

"Tell you what, Tonia," Julie said, bending down to speak to the little girl at her own level. "You can make a bunch of those calico bags you sew so well. And we'll stuff them with dried beans for the bean-bag toss. Okay?" Tonia nodded happily and skipped away to begin sewing, and when Julie straightened, she was face-to-face with Stephen.

"Has anyone ever told you that you are very good with children?" he said pleasantly. A smile played around his lips, inviting further conversation.

But Julie, taken by surprise, said something like, "Um, well, yes. Er, no." She fled, feeling like a fool. All he had done was pay her a compliment, and she had fallen apart. She couldn't even speak two words in sequence; he must think she was a prize idiot.

As for Stephen, he didn't think she was an idiot. He thought she cared for him more than she was willing to admit. Why else would she lose her composure when he spoke to her? He cautioned himself to remain patient. Only if she trusted him and felt comfortable around him would she ever confide in him, and lately Julie didn't seem comfortable around anyone.

Everyone was up early on the Fourth, holiday or not. Julie brushed aside the curtain of her room, to see puffs of cotton-candy clouds dotting a china-blue sky, and she greeted the day with almost as much enthusiasm as she had when she was a child. Then, too, all the cousins had always been together, and every year they'd staged their own big picnic. The Fourth of July had always been a special day for the Andrassys, so recently arrived in this country. After their escape from Hungary, they had counted themselves fortunate to be able to celebrate it.

After breakfast, Julie tacked her schedule of events on the front of the refrigerator with a daisy-shaped magnet.

"Ten o'clock—three-legged race," Sam read, standing in front of the refrigerator and munching on a doughnut.

"Eleven o'clock—sack race," Eric said. "Hmm, I bet I can win that one."

"What time is the beanbag toss?" Tonia wanted to know. "I made the beanbags myself."

At that point, Stephen rushed into the kitchen.

"I haven't missed anything, have I?"

"No, but where have you been?" chorused the children.

"Down at the meadow, practicing."

"I thought you said I should never practice on the wire by myself. You said I should always have someone there in case I fall," Sam said.

"It is different for me," Stephen said.

"Is it?" Julie asked pointedly. "Is it?"

Stephen shot Julie a sharp look. He hoped that she wasn't going to ruin their holiday. She wouldn't do it intentionally, but—

The kids, caught up in the excitement of the day, all disappeared at once, leaving Stephen and Julie alone in the kitchen.

Julie put a carton of milk back into the refrigerator. Stephen opened the refrigerator and took it out again. He poured some into a glass.

Julie closed the box of doughnuts and set them on a cupboard shelf. Stephen opened the cupboard and took the doughnuts out again. He stood and watched her, chewing thoughtfully on his doughnut.

Julie dropped a box of eggs. It flew open and the eggs spattered all over the kitchen floor. She looked down at the eggs, their slimy whites and yolks smearing the clean vinyl tile, and covered her face with her hands. She burst into tears.

Even though she was sobbing, Julie knew that Stephen knelt and cleaned up the mess with a damp rag.

She heard him toss the broken egg shells into the garbage container. She went on crying as though her heart would break.

"It is more than the eggs, is it not?" he said quietly when he thought her tears had stopped. Julie breathed damply through her fingers. She didn't want him to see her face. She pressed her fingertips into her eyeballs, willing the tears not to start again.

"Yes," she said at last.

"For God's sake, Juliana, don't keep everything pent-up inside you. You're like a walking time bomb, waiting to go off. We all tiptoe around you, careful not to say anything, careful not to do anything to upset Julie. We are on guard all the time. How long can you expect a family to go on like that?"

Shocked at the accusatory tone in his voice, Julie dropped her hands and stared at him. She had never heard Stephen speak in anything but his own gentle fashion.

He passed a hand over his eyes as though just realizing what he had said.

"I am sorry," he said heavily. "We won't talk about our work on the wire if you don't wish us to." He tossed the rag in the garbage can and started to stride from the room.

"Stephen," Julie said urgently. "Wait!"

He turned slowly, eyebrows lifted.

"I—I don't want you all to be so...considerate of me. I wish you would all act normal."

He came back and stood in front of her. He looked at her for a long time before he spoke. And when he spoke, the words were uttered with warmth and gentleness.

"Juliana, if we acted normal, we would talk freely about our work. We would speak of Tallulah Gorge. But none of us want to see the look on your face when we mention those things. None of us want to be responsible for making your face go pale, for making you run out of the room."

His expression was open, sincere and honest. He was telling her how he felt about something that was very important to him. She longed to respond in kind, but all she could do was stare up at him mutely, unable to give him any assurance that she wouldn't go rigid when anyone mentioned walking the wire, that she wouldn't flee from any room where the work of the Andrassys was being discussed.

Finally Stephen shook his head, his expression tender but rueful. "It is all right, Juliana. I am sorry I said those things to you. I know you cannot help it. Come, I will help you get ready for the—what is it?" He looked around and consulted the list on the refrigerator. "Yes, the three-legged race."

"You don't have to," she murmured, brushing a tear from her cheek.

"No, I don't have to. But I *want* to, Juliana. Come." He held his hand out to her. How could she not take it?

And so they left the house, hand in hand. Julie couldn't remember anyone being this nice to her, ever. In spite of everything, it was, she reflected, going to be very difficult to say goodbye to Stephen at the end of the summer—very difficult indeed.

AFTER THE THREE-LEGGED RACE and the beanbag toss and the sack race, after the big dinner with fried chicken and Nonna's special potato-and-cucumber salad, they gathered at night in the meadow for fire-works.

Julie passed out sparklers to everyone. Tonia chased fireflies. Nonna complained that she had to sit in a webbed lawn chair while everyone else lounged on widely scattered blankets brought to the meadow from the house.

Paul set up torches around the meadow for illumination, which they really didn't need once Michael and Sam and Eric began to set off the fireworks they had bought.

The first one was a Roman candle, which made a loud *pop*. Then followed a spate of red-white-and-blue fountains to splash the sky with light.

"It is so beautiful," Stephen said in awe. He sat down next to Julie on her blanket and leaned back on one arm. If she were to lean back, too, she would touch his arm. Warm ripples cascaded down her spine at the thought.

"Is the Fourth of July always so much fun?" Stephen asked, his lips so close to her ear that they stirred the little tendrils of her hair. She longed to move closer, to make his lips brush her ear. She closed her eyes and fought the empty sensation in the pit of her stomach.

"Well, is it?" he asked, and she opened her eyes again, wondering how she could ever have forgotten the question he had just asked her.

She hitched herself a few inches further away from him. "Our family has always made a big deal about the Fourth," she replied.

She heard a humming sound in the vicinity of her neck, but just then a starburst of shimmering gold flakes lit up the sky, and she ignored the humming in order to ooh and ahh with everyone else.

"There!" said Stephen, bringing his hand down solidly on her shoulder. "I am sorry, Juliana, but there was a mosquito."

She turned her head. His soft blue eyes gazed deep into hers, and he didn't remove his hand. Her lips parted and she couldn't look away. He was staring at her as though he were memorizing every eyelash, every contour, every nuance of expression. Her breath seemed to leave her lungs.

"Ooh," said everyone else. "Ahh." Above them a glittering sunburst shimmered in midair and hung suspended before its silvery confetti drifted to earth.

"Dearest Juliana," Stephen said helplessly. Her eyes widened as she watched his lips float slowly down to hers. They lingered there briefly, sending shocks of electricity through her body. The world seemed to stop; she didn't even hear the crackle of the fireworks as they went off, and her heart forgot to beat. Then a dazzling golden glow lit up the sky and Julie remembered where they were and who was there, and she leaned away from him a bit, watching his rapt face gilded in the light from the sky.

"You know what would make this perfect?" Eric yelled. "If Stephen would go up on the wire while we set off these last fireworks!"

Stephen removed his hand from her shoulder and Julie was swept by a cold chill.

"Will you, Stephen? Will you perform for us?" Nonna leaned forward in her lawn chair.

"Well, I—" Stephen glanced at Julie, looking extremely uncomfortable. What would she think, what would she do if he left her now to climb up on the wire?

"Please, Stephen," Mickey begged. "I want to see you do it."

Well, why not? It would be a private show for his family, his own family, and when Julie saw him on the wire, finally saw him doing what he did best, maybe she would forget her fear for him. Maybe he could convince her, not with words but by doing, that he felt safe and at home in the air.

"I will," he said quietly, and he leaped up from where he sat and ran toward the high wire erected not forty feet away.

"His shoes," Julie murmured. The Andrassys wore soft buffalo-hide slippers, not unlike ballet shoes, on the wire.

But Stephen discarded his Docksiders and climbed the ladder in his bare feet. He wore a pair of shorts and a T-shirt; he wasn't dressed to perform. Nevertheless, he looked very much at home on the platform.

In the light of the torches he looked determined and yet somehow lighthearted, chin thrust forward, testing the wind for its direction.

Behind him, Julie saw Sam set off another fountain firework, this one with a whistle. And then two other fountains, red and blue, soared high into the sky.

Stephen did not use a balancing pole. He stepped confidently onto the wire, gazing intently at the cable stretched before him. He balanced, first on one bare foot, next on the other. Julie bit down hard on her lip to keep from crying out, but even as her emotions battled for control, her intellect told her that she had nothing to fear.

Stephen on the wire was supple and sure. He moved effortlessly to midwire, then stopped and knelt, raising his arms in one graceful movement, a classic wire walker's salute. When he stood, his body was strong and erect, and he completed his crossing as the last fireworks sputtered and popped and lit the sky in one final beautiful tribute to America's independence. And Julie knew that Stephen's walk on the wire on this Fourth of July night was his tribute to his own independence.

"Now that wasn't so bad, Julie, was it?" Paul said, speaking quietly to her as they gathered up their blankets.

She shook her head, unable to speak, and hurried from the meadow hard on the heels of the capering children, so that she wouldn't have to say anything to Stephen, who walked behind her with Eva and Susan and stared at the back of her neck all the way back to the house.

THE MONDAY AFTER the Fourth of July weekend, the house was overrun with people. The producer of the television show *Thrills!* announced in a press release that Stephen Andrassy was going to cross the Tallulah Gorge on a cable. Network people, newspaper people, wire service people, press-agent people all descended on the farm. And they stayed, and stayed.

A reporter met Julie in the driveway one morning when she was running and jogged along beside her, holding out one of those tiny battery-operated tape recorders to catch her every word. What was he like, the Soviet defector, Stephen Martinovic-Andrassy? Was he her cousin? Why wasn't she practicing with the others? And by the way, what did Stephen eat for breakfast?

The reporter didn't get his money's worth. Julie barely said a word. After that incident she began to vary the times when she ran, so that her habits wouldn't be predictable. She didn't want to be caught in that position again.

Stephen, however, seemed to glory in all the attention. He granted interviews, talking at length about his work with the Moscow Circus, about his stint with the Big Apple Circus. He demonstrated his art on the high wire in the meadow for photographers. He handed out publicity photos and biographical sheets. Whenever possible, he included other members of the Amazing Andrassys in the pictures.

"You're getting quite famous," Julie couldn't help observing tartly one night after Stephen had bade goodbye to a reporter from *TV Times*. She was sitting on the front porch, enjoying a cool breeze. Stephen sat down in a chair beside her.

"If I am getting famous, that is good," he said solemnly.

"You love it, don't you? You thrive on the attention."

Stephen laughed. "I suppose I do, Juliana. One works to get to the top of a profession, and it is gratifying to be recognized as the best. Tell me, does it annoy you, my being famous?"

Julie considered the question thoughtfully. "It's like living in a goldfish bowl," she answered truthfully. "Everyone is always following us around. But, Stephen, you should know that I *am* proud of you."

"You don't like what I do, but you are proud of me." He broke into a smile. "I think I like that, Juliana. Yes, I like that very much." He stopped smiling, assuming a more serious expression. He reached over the gap between their chairs and touched her cheek, running a forefinger along the curve of her jawbone.

"I feel very lucky to have you for my friend," he said softly.

Julie had the breathless feeling that he might kiss her, but at that moment they heard the approach of a car and Stephen self-consciously removed his hand.

The car was a small blue one, and it discharged Mimi Fitchett, a publicity assistant from *Thrills!* It didn't help matters, from Julie's point of view, that Mimi, who had visited briefly once before, was young, pretty and wore a very short skirt.

"Are you Stephen? Stephen Andrassy?" Mimi called, squinting at him through the dim illumination of the yellow porch light.

"Yes, I am," Stephen said, standing up.

"Well, I wasn't due here until tomorrow, but I got through with my business in Chicago today and decided to fly in tonight. Is there a decent motel around here anywhere?" She yanked a briefcase off the front seat and began to walk purposefully toward the house.

Of course, there was no motel in Peaceable Kingdom, and so Stephen went inside to telephone a motel in nearby Gainesville to reserve Ms. Fitchett a room.

Mimi stayed on the porch with Julie, flicking orange flecks of fingernail polish off her nails and shooting curious glances in Julie's direction. Julie continued to sit in her rocking chair, rocking gently in time to the mournful rhythm of the crickets. Through the open window she could hear Stephen making Mimi's motel reservation.

"I guess you're the Andrassy who doesn't perform," Mimi said after a while.

Julie stopped rocking and stared at her. An inexplicable heaviness settled around her heart, and she felt a twinge of longing for the old days when she had been proud when people recognized her as Juliana Andrassy, the youngest member of the Amazing Andrassys performing troupe.

But those days were gone forever.

"Yes," Julie said quietly. "I'm the Andrassy who doesn't perform."

And excusing herself, she slipped quickly into the house before Stephen could return.

Chapter Nine

Excitement in the household increased as the date of Stephen's Tallulah Gorge crossing drew near. Stephen, Paul, Albert and Michael spent many days at the Gorge installing the rigging, a process that would take weeks and that invaded every aspect of their daily lives.

Practice on the high wire in the meadow was curtailed. Julie, out for her run at all hours of the day and night, grew accustomed to stumbling over piles of rope and stacks of steel cable on the front porch of the farmhouse. Stephen walked around looking preoccupied and wearing a heavy leather belt with loops and pockets for tools, the kind of belt a telephone lineman would wear. The belt and its tools were, Julie knew, the tools of Stephen's trade as much as the wire and his balancing pole.

"We can use the steel pylon on the south side of the Gorge. Karl Wallenda used the same pylon for his rigging when he crossed in 1970," Stephen told them all enthusiastically after one of his first long days at the site. "It's still in good shape. We're installing a new pylon on the north side, where I will begin my walk."

"They're building a big covered observation deck near the place where Stephen will end his walk. It's for local dignitaries. And family, of course," Michael added.

"Do you know they're expecting at least twenty-five thousand people to watch Stephen walk across the Tallulah Gorge?" Paul said in amazement. "Twenty-five thousand people! Isn't that something?"

Julie steeled herself for more of the same kind of talk, but now she was determined not to make the members of her family feel awkward around her. Stephen was right. She shouldn't cause them to feel uneasy about a walk that, in family annals, would go down as a great achievement. As best she could, she hid her worry from everyone.

"The producer of *Thrills!* has rented a big house in the mountains not far from the Gorge," Stephen announced at dinner one evening. "I, of course, will live in the house for a few days before the crossing, so I can supervise last-minute adjustments to the rigging. The rest of you can spend the night before the crossing there. We're free to use the house for the rest of the week if we want."

"A vacation!" Susan exclaimed. "We need a vacation."

The others were enthusiastic about staying at the mountain house, but Julie greeted Stephen's announcement in silence. She didn't plan to go to Tallulah Gorge at all. She'd stay at the farmhouse, far away from Stephen and his performance.

"Won't you change your mind?" Stephen asked later that night when they met accidentally on the stairs. He wrinkled his forehead. "I'd like you to be at the Gorge for my walk, Juliana."

Julie shook her head, afraid to speak out loud. Stephen stared at her for a moment, his face torn with frustration, before Julie brushed past him toward her room. She looked out her window and saw him heading for the meadow alone, his path illumined only by the cold glare of the moon; she wanted to do something to ease his pain, but she knew there was nothing she could do.

The countdown began—a week to go, then six days, then five. The producer of *Thrills!* called at the farmhouse and electrified the performing troupe by hinting that if they'd all walk across Tallulah Gorge during the next television season, he'd put their family act on his show. A story about Stephen's planned crossing appeared in *People* magazine. A European film crew arrived to make a documentary of the walk.

Then there were only four days to go. The next day Stephen would leave for the house in the mountains to prepare for his walk.

Stephen was in his room when Julie mounted the stairs late that night while the rest of the household slept. She'd been out jogging in the moonlight, running as though something was chasing her. She hadn't, she reflected as she reached the top of the stairs, managed to outrun it.

"Juliana?" When he saw her, Stephen looked up from a magazine he was reading. He had been waiting for her; he'd heard the light click of her door latch when she'd left, and he'd watched her from his window as she set off running down the moonlit driveway. He'd been waiting for a long time for an opportunity to speak with her privately.

Julie walked slowly to his door and stood gazing down at him. She tried not to look at the clothes spread out on the back of the couch: scarlet tights, white satin breeches, a blue fringed sash, white buffalo-hide slippers. A scarlet-lined white satin cape hung in gleaming splendor from the closet door. These clothes were what Stephen would wear for his crossing of the Gorge.

Stephen drank in Julie's beauty like one too long deprived. It seemed that he never saw her away from the others these days. He had missed her.

"Come in," he invited, patting the couch beside him. "We haven't talked in a long time."

"You've had so much to do," she said. She sat down beside him and pulled one of the couch's small pillows into her lap, holding it in front of her like a shield. She played with a loose piece of appliquéd design, feeling out of place. She'd never visited Stephen alone in his room before.

"Soon the crossing will be over," he said with satisfaction. "Then I will have more free time."

"I doubt it. You'll go back to training every day, won't you?"

"Yes, we will. We have a lot to learn before September."

"You're not going to attempt a pyramid when you go back on the wire with the others?" She hadn't wanted to ask, but she felt compelled to.

"We could do a five-person pyramid. But to do the wonderful nine-person Andrassy pyramid—it will be years before we can attempt it. We don't have enough people."

"But you will someday, is that it?"

"If Sam keeps up his work with us, and if Eric joins us, and if later Mickey and Tonia want to be a part of the act, then we will do the nine-person pyramid." His expression was calm.

"So Sam is hooked on the high wire, is he?" murmured Julie bitterly.

"He shows much talent, yes."

Julie sighed. "Really, Stephen, I must go to bed now. I'm very tired."

"I knew you would not approve of my plans for the act," Stephen said slowly. "But I don't want to keep them from you."

"What difference does it make whether I know your plans or not?"

"It is important to me for you to know everything about me," he said in a low tone. "Everything."

Julie stiffened, not knowing how to take this.

"Just as important," he went on, "as it is for me to know everything about you. Don't you know why, Juliana? Haven't you guessed?"

She stared at him dumbly, afraid for both of them. Some words were best left unspoken.

"Juliana, I am leaving tomorrow for the mountains to undertake a very dangerous mission. I am confident that I will make a successful crossing of the Gorge, but I am never unaware of the dangers, even though you might think I am. I think it is best for you to know what is in my mind and in my heart."

"Not here—not now," she whispered.

"Ah, do you think this cramped little sewing room is not quite the romantic place?" His mouth quirked upward in a brief flash of humor.

"Well, I—"

"Believe me, Juliana, I would much prefer it if we could sit on the banks of the creek in the moonlight, as we did one other time. Or if we were eating dinner by candlelight, just you and me. But there has been no opportunity for such frivolous things, and somehow I think it doesn't matter. I think that we are both very practical in some ways and that romantic trappings would not make that much difference.''

Julie didn't know what to say. Stephen's talk of moonlit creek banks and candlelight dinners was unexpected, and at the moment those situations didn't seem at all romantic. What seemed romantic right now was that the two of them were entirely alone, face-to-face, that they were able to speak what was in their minds and in their hearts without preliminaries, and that, somehow, despite Stephen's obsession with the wire and her own aversion to it, they understood each other on a deeply human level.

"Many times I have thought of your face glowing up at me in the moonlight, or of making love to you— no, let me finish!"

Julie stirred restlessly, hugging the couch pillow even closer. His words seemed inappropriate, but were they? They were surely no more inappropriate than her body's swift response to the sweetly yearning expression in his eyes and the gentle smile that played about his lips. She longed to touch his face, to kiss his lips. Not touching him seemed like exquisite torture; she remembered so well that night in her car when they had stopped just short of unchecked passion. She felt her cheeks grow hot with the memory.

"I *have* dreamed of making love to you, Juliana. Many, many times. But knowing how you feel about what I do for a living, I have been afraid to care for you too deeply. And I have been afraid for you to care for me. Yet I think you care for me more than you let on.''

He paused, wishing she would speak. Her luminous dark eyes refused to leave his face, and her lips were moist and slightly parted. She looked fearful and yet somehow relieved, and so he plunged on, groping for the right words. English was not his native language, but it was the only language Julie understood. He must say this right.

"You need not tell me your feelings, Juliana, if you don't wish to. But I must tell you mine. Please believe me when I tell you that I love you."

Her rapid intake of breath interrupted him, and he gently took the couch pillow from her and let it fall to the floor. Then he reached out and pushed the door quietly shut and clasped her hands in his. Her hands trembled like two frightened birds.

"Yes, Juliana, I do love you. And I must add that loving is not something I do often," he said, smiling to reassure her.

"I don't know why you are telling me this," breathed Julie.

"Because if anything happens to me, I would want you to know that Stephen Andrassy truly loved you. That is why."

In her mind's eye, Julie pictured Stephen setting out on the wire over the great Tallulah Gorge, sliding one foot forward, then the other, his balancing pole shifting carefully from side to side, helping him to keep his balance. He was concentrating mightily on the wire, an expression of intensity on his face, and it was so far until he would reach the other side, so very far....

"I can't bear it," she blurted out. "I can't stand to think about it!"

"About my love?" Stephen said, holding fast to her hands. "So now I have made my great declaration and you cannot stand to think about it. Dearest Juliana, do you have any idea how that makes me feel?" He was teasing her.

"No, no, the Gorge! You treat it so lightly, as though it's nothing, but how do you think I'll feel when I know you're out there, suspended in space? Stephen, how can you put me through this?"

"It is the way I live. I'm made to walk the wire. It is all in a day's work, as you Americans would say." He grinned at her, but then he became serious once more. He remembered how he had felt in the aftermath of the tornado. Because he had already admitted to himself that he couldn't have borne it if anything had happened to Julie, he could identify with the fear she felt right now.

"Don't do it, Stephen! Please! Call it off. Please?"

"There is no way I can do that," he said quietly. When she didn't reply, he drew a deep breath and continued.

"Juliana, I would like to think that someday there might be a chance for us to have a life together. This is why I have told you how I feel about you. Do you— do you think it would ever be possible for you to love me?" He held his breath, watching her face. Many expressions flitted across it in rapid succession— longing, sorrow, hope, affection. But he didn't find any acceptance there.

"I don't think I could have a future with a man who walks the wire," murmured Julie, looking down at the floor.

He tipped a finger beneath her chin and forced her eyes to meet his.

"But you care, don't you? Admit it, Juliana! You care for me as I care for you, do you not?" His eyes cut into her like chips of blue glass.

Slowly she slipped her hands from his fierce grasp, and slowly she slid them up his chest, over his solid pectoral muscles, to his shoulders and the nape of his neck. Her fingers tangled in the straight silky hair there and she closed her eyes. When she opened them again, his expressive face was only inches from hers, and she lifted her lips to be kissed.

He stroked her hair reverently; his arms pulled her close until her body touched his. All her senses seemed enhanced, and a quiet exhilaration made her heart leap with happiness. He bent his head until their lips touched, and then she was clasping him to her as though she would never, ever let him go. Awareness of him flowed through her, awareness of his lean, strong muscles urging her closer and closer, of his lips, so warm and passionate, evoking a long-denied greed.

His kisses carried her to a place where she had never been before, a place where the pulse of her blood was the only sound, a place where the intensity of this moment pushed all other considerations out of her mind. Repressed instincts flared, and long-forgotten responses surged through her. His arms tightened, crushing her to his chest. She heard his heartbeat and mistook it for her own.

Her body seemed inhabited by someone else, and yet it was more hers than ever because it had never been so sensitive to sensation before. And now that this body of hers seemed so real, so alive, she wanted nothing more than to give it away—to him.

His lips blistered her throat and feathered soft little kisses on her temple; they burned a trail along her

jawline and lovingly tasted of her mouth. His hands
fumbled with the band holding her ponytail, and her
hair cascaded in all its splendor to make a silky curtain over her face. Slowly he caressed it and drew it
back over one ear, weaving his fingers through its
sumptuous length.

"When I think of making love to you, it is with your
hair down, like this," he whispered, his breath burning her cheek.

She took his other hand in hers and lifted it slowly
until that hand, too, threaded through the heavy fall
of her hair. He slowly wound the lustrous tresses in his
hands, finally cupping his hands on either side of her
head. He steadied her head for a moment and then,
with delectable slowness, he brought his lips to hers.

Her mouth blossomed beneath his, and the only
thought she had was what incredible pleasure it was to
feel the physical closeness of another. She dimly felt
one of his hands as it slowly came up to cup her breast.
His lips slipped down and down, leaving her gasping,
until his cheek rested against the gentle curve. An
aching tightness curled in her abdomen as he pressed
his lips to the soft peak, and she heard herself moan
deep in her throat.

He unbuttoned the knit shirt she wore until she was
bare to his gaze, and his soft intake of breath at the
sight of her made her weak with pleasure. She was
small, very small, too small to bother wearing a bra,
but she saw in his eyes that he found her beautiful.

His fingertips traced the shape of her breasts,
touching them gently, wonderingly. "You are so
lovely," he said, and his voice was hoarse. "You are
perfect, do you know that?" He lifted his eyes and
raised one hand to touch her hair. "Your hair, dark as

midnight, and your beautiful dusky skin, and your lips, so full and well-fitted to mine. And your breasts, they are the perfect shape. I have never admired big-breasted women, Juliana, do you know that? I like a woman to be softly rounded there, like you."

His golden lashes drifted closed as he touched his lips to one dark peak, and as his warm mouth engulfed her, she felt an intoxicating sense of power. Overwhelmed, she let her head fall forward and buried her face in his pale, shining hair, inhaling the warm, new-mown-hay scent of him until she was nearly drunk with it.

She fell gracefully backward until she lay against the couch cushions, drawing him with her. His breathing came faster, grew more rapid, and she was gasping, too, arching under him, wanting to be free of her clothes. But he was too heavy, she couldn't reach the buttons, and she frantically tried to lift the shirt he wore over his head. She longed for him; she needed him. The stiffening of his body came as a complete surprise.

In one fierce motion, his arms went around her and pressed her to him, and his breathing slowed against her neck.

"Stephen?" she murmured, not believing that he was calling a halt.

He drew her head down and kissed her gently on the lips. "This time we came so close," he whispered. "So very close."

Her breathing slowed, and she struggled with her emotions. Neither of them spoke, but they remained wrapped in each other's arms, letting the rhythm of their bodies slowly return to normal.

"Why did you want to stop?" she asked after a time, blinking back sudden stinging tears.

"I didn't want to," he said. "But I am not willing to put you through an emotional crisis for which you are not ready."

Julie struggled upright, carefully avoiding touching Stephen's costume, which lay across the back of the couch. Stephen sat up too. He cradled her in his arms and sprinkled little kisses along the side of her neck.

He straightened and pulled slightly away. "I love you very much," he said, his eyes darkening. Now he watched her steadily, and his voice held a note of authority.

"Then why—?"

"I know you care for me. I see it in your eyes. No, do not turn away, look at me."

Julie forced herself to raise her eyelids. Stephen's expression was one of fervent hope.

"Someday you will be able to tell me that you love me. I love you enough to offer you a life with me. I want to marry you, Juliana."

The joy she had felt evaporated, leaving only a bitter residue of sadness.

"You know how I feel about your walking the wire," she said unhappily.

"Yes, I know. And I cannot spend my life making you unhappy. All I want to do is to make you happy, Juliana. If I cannot do that, I will not marry you."

"Dear God," she said helplessly. "What are you saying, Stephen?"

"That I can only marry you if you accept my life on the wire. It is the only life I know and the only life I want. I would like to share it with you."

"And tonight?"

"Tonight I wanted to make love to you, but it is harder to say goodbye to a lover than to a friend. I do not want to make it harder for you, Juliana, if your answer must be no." He smiled and raised a tender finger to brush a tear from her cheek, and then he kissed the place where it had been.

"Nonna always says a kiss makes it better," he said lightly.

"It would take a lot of kisses to make this better," Julie said, smiling wryly in spite of the ache in her heart. She didn't see how their love could be resolved satisfactorily for either of them.

Stephen chuckled deep in his throat and pulled her close. Then he picked her shirt up from the floor and helped her put it on. When it was buttoned, he held her silently for a few moments, gently caressing the nape of her neck.

"Go to bed, Juliana," he whispered in her ear. "To your own bed. You must believe I love you, if I love you enough to let you go now."

She stood up and so did he; then she wrapped her arms around him and hugged him tight. She'd never thought she was capable of loving a man so much.

"You are my friend," she said in a broken voice. "My very good friend."

"Even when I am your husband, I intend to be your friend," he said.

In desperation Julie said, "Oh, Stephen, why weren't you good at—at fixing cars or—or making widgets, or building highways? Why did you have to be good at walking a wire?"

It was only a rhetorical question. But Stephen took it seriously.

"Because, Juliana," he said quietly, "I was meant to touch the stars."

THE FARMHOUSE WAS QUIET. Everyone had left—the performing troupe the night before, and Stephen had left for the mountains before that. Carol, Nonna, Sam, Eric and Linda and the two children had just driven out of the driveway in two cars, headed for Tallulah Gorge. Stephen would begin his walk across the Gorge at two o'clock.

The morning heat on this mid-August Saturday was stifling, and Julie gave up the idea of running a couple of miles. At loose ends, she went inside the house, picking up one of Tonia's Barbie dolls here, emptying a wastebasket there. It was so quiet with everyone gone!

Julie realized with a jolt that she had never been alone in the farmhouse. Someone had always been around. Her footsteps echoed hollowly on the wooden floor of the hall, which made her feel even more depressed. As keyed up as she was over the crossing, how on earth was she going to get through this day?

Stephen had asked her one last time before he got into the car on the morning he had left, and she had told him again that she would not come to watch him walk the Tallulah Gorge. She didn't think she could bear to watch; it would be the utmost torture to see him out there on the wire, suspended over jagged rocks and trees and—well, just to think of it made her stomach heave. She folded her arms across her abdomen and sat down listlessly in front of the television set. If only someone had stayed behind to keep her company! But no one had offered, and she felt more than a little self-pity. She turned the TV on, thinking that maybe there'd be something that would catch her interest.

She watched a few minutes of an award-winning documentary about homeless people, and then came a station break. During the station break the singer-actress Rose O'Sharon appeared to plug her new movie, and an announcer from *Thrills!* informed the viewers that Rose O'Sharon would make a personal appearance to sing the national anthem at Tallulah Gorge at two o'clock, when the famous high-wire performer, Stephen Andrassy, was going to walk a two-inch steel cable across the—

Julie snapped the television set off. She pressed her fists into her eyes, and her breath ripped out of her in great sobs. No matter what she did today, she couldn't get away from it. Stephen was going to walk across the Tallulah Gorge, and whether she was there in person or not, she would be there in her thoughts. She loved him, and she would be wherever Stephen Andrassy went, no matter what he did, because he was always in her heart and in her mind.

Feverishly Julie leaped to her feet and ran upstairs. She found a canvas tote bag and stuffed her nightgown and a spare set of clothes into it; she scooped her few cosmetics from the dresser. She stopped by the bathroom and grabbed her toothbrush, and then she ran down the stairs two at a time. She slammed the front door, pausing only long enough to make sure she had locked it behind her.

She was in her car, lurching it into gear, wheeling it around until she was on the driveway, going lickety-split. Frantically she thought of the last-minute preparations for Stephen's walk. She remembered them all so well from her own days on the wire.

Stephen would be kicking at the anchors for the cavallettis, testing them for strength. He would be rappeling down the walls of the Gorge, checking the cable from underneath to see if it leaned to either the right or left. His personal preparations would include pulling on his stirrup tights, making sure that they did not bind his foot uncomfortably. He would be roughing up the soles of his buffalo-hide slippers with a special file, and he would be pulling on his satin breeches. He would thrust his feet into wooden clogs that fit loosely over his slippers. Finally, he would flip his scarlet-lined cape over his shoulders, the cape she had seen hanging on the closet door in the sewing room. And Julie would not be there.

She was leaving the big empty farmhouse because she could not stay there alone. She had to be present when Stephen stepped off the high wire after a successful crossing. She could not let him cross the Gorge without her being there.

It would be hard for her to watch him; it would be terrifying. She didn't know how she would be able to stand it when she watched Stephen out on the wire, advancing slowly toward her. She didn't know how she would be able to look down, down into the yawning chasm when Stephen was suspended over it.

But she would be there. Anything would be better than being back in the farmhouse, all alone, while thousands of other people watched Stephen cross the treacherous Tallulah Gorge with nothing between him and death but a two-inch steel cable.

Chapter Ten

The town of Tallulah Falls was, well, *engorged* with visitors, Julie thought distractedly as she dodged battered pickup trucks and Cadillacs and a Subaru that had no sense of direction. She fought for a parking place, lost it, and was finally urged to park in a vacant lot by a boy who was collecting five dollars apiece from drivers desperate to find a space to park.

"Where do I go to watch the crossing?" she asked hurriedly as she pressed a five-dollar bill into his hand, and the boy said, "There's a bus to take you there." So Julie hopped onto a minivan already occupied by several other passengers, including a baby who wailed at the top of his lungs. They jounced the short distance to Tallulah Point, the same place where she and Stephen had come to see the Gorge, and she jumped out of the minivan into a street-carnival atmosphere.

She looked for an observation deck—Michael had said there would be an observation deck. Julie glanced both ways before attempting to cross the busy street, and an impatient policeman directing traffic waved her back. She retreated obediently, backing into a fat man hawking programs. She bought a program and asked the man, "Where's the observation deck, the one for visiting dignitaries?"

"I dunno, miss," he said. "I just sell programs."

A girl vending balloons with a picture of Stephen's face on them overheard the exchange and told Julie, "It's down that way." She pointed toward the dirt road where Stephen had driven them the day of their outing, and where Julie had watched the family having a tailgate picnic while Stephen got out of the car and looked around.

She fought her way through the throng, and someone stepped on her foot. She barely felt the pain. All she could think about was getting to the observation deck. That was the only important thing now.

The dirt road abounded with milling people. It led to an area on the south side of the Gorge from which the public could watch the crossing, and through the overlying haze of dust, Julie saw a flag-bedecked, canvas-roofed structure that she assumed was the observation deck. The path to it was blocked off by police barricades where two policemen stood guard.

A woman carrying a baby in a blue canvas sling jostled Julie, apologized and hurried on. A troop of Boy Scouts ran past, and she was caught up in their midst. In the free-for-all, the ribbon holding her hair in its ponytail came untied and fell to the ground, where it was trampled in the dust along with the bright skins of popped balloons. She heard a band warming up, and frantically she realized that Stephen's walk was about to begin. If she didn't hurry, she would be too late.

"Excuse me," Julie said, approaching one of the police officers standing at the barricade. "I need to go to the observation deck."

"The only people allowed past this point are authorized visitors. You got a pass?"

"No, but I'm Julie Andrassy. The wire walker's . . . cousin," she said. She thought she would be more believable if she claimed to be a relative of Stephen's.

The policeman stared at her. "You don't look like him," he said.

"I got a twin brother, and we don't look nothing alike," the other policeman said, smiling at her.

Julie pushed her hair back behind her ears. "Please," she said urgently, addressing the smiling policeman. "I've got to get through. The rest of my family is there, and we got separated, but I'm supposed to be with them. Really, I am." She favored him with her sweetest smile.

"Well, I dunno," he said doubtfully.

The band, warmed up now, began to play "The Star Spangled Banner." Julie heard the full-throated voice of Rose O'Sharon. If she didn't get there soon, she would be too late.

"Here," she said desperately, digging in her handbag. She found her wallet and flipped through all the family pictures to her driver's license. "See? Juliana Andrassy, that's me."

The nice policeman blew a bubble with blue bubble gum and popped it between his teeth. He studied the picture on her driver's license for what seemed like years.

"Okay, lady, you can go through. But just this once, y'hear?" He winked at her, hoping she understood his joke. She did, but she didn't have time to laugh. She only had time to run, and run she did, sprinting toward the observation deck where she could see, through a fine mist of dust around the pylon that anchored the wire, Paul's burly back and Linda's bright red hair.

Yet another policeman tried to bar her way onto the observation deck, but Linda caught sight of her and before she knew it, Paul and Sam were reaching down and pulling her up onto the stand.

"You came!" Linda said, looking surprised. Tonia squealed and jumped up and down at the sight of Julie.

"Now we're all here," Tonia said happily.

Nonna turned stiffly around in her chair at the front of the deck. "I am so glad you are here, Julie," she said approvingly.

"I couldn't stay away," Julie explained, her words tumbling out in rapid succession. Paul looked at her strangely, and suddenly she realized why. She must look wild, with her hair tumbling down her back. "The ribbon fell out of my hair," she said, impatiently pushing her hair back.

"It looks fine," Paul said, as though seeing her in a new light. "You should wear it like that more often."

Julie ignored this remark. "It's a zoo out there," she said, gesturing back at the crowd. "There are all these people rushing around, and they have balloons with Stephen's picture on them and—"

"I know, but it's good publicity," Eva said. "Come on. Come stand with Susan and me. We're way over in the corner, with a good view of the platform on the north side of the Gorge."

"What's happening?" Julie asked, craning for a view across the chasm. The optical illusion of the Gorge's north wall bending toward her had not diminished; instinctively she reeled backward.

"This morning there was square dancing, and we had a barbecue at noon where Stephen signed autographs." Eva was interrupted while they bowed their heads for an invocation. Julie saw Rose O'Sharon on the stage at the other side of the viewing area; after the minister had finished praying, the star stepped into a dove-gray limousine and was driven away. The uniformed brass band played the *Thrills!* jumpy theme song and the announcer from the show took control of the microphone.

"Where's Stephen?" Julie asked urgently. She hadn't seen him yet.

"He's on the other side of the Gorge," Carol explained. "Albert and Michael are with him."

The announcer then called out, "Ladies and gentlemen, the moment you have all been waiting for is about to begin. Stephen Andrassy is about to start his treacherous walk across the magnificent Tallulah Gorge. In case some of you are not familiar with the name Andrassy, let me tell you about this illustrious family." The announcer kept talking, his words reverberating loudly from the strategically placed loudspeakers around the viewing area.

"Do you have an extra pair of binoculars?" Julie asked nervously. She didn't care to listen to the family history the *Thrills!* announcer was outlining.

"Here, use these. I brought them for Mickey, but he doesn't like them." Linda handed her a pair of lightweight binoculars, and Julie held them up to her eyes. They brought the pylon on the other side of the chasm startlingly close.

There was a flurry of movement in the woods surrounding the pylon, and Julie, ignoring the shimmering optical illusion of the walls, identified Michael in the group of photographers and TV cameramen waiting for Stephen to mount the wire.

"Do you see him? Do you, do you?" Tonia asked.

"Not yet," Julie replied automatically. She focused the binoculars on the wire. It swayed ever so slightly with the capricious wind sweeping down the Gorge, but to Julie's practiced eye, the cavallettis seemed well-placed and tight. Below the cable swooped banks of power lines strung between poles. If Stephen fell, chances were he'd become entangled in them. Julie's stomach cramped at the thought.

"Stephen Andrassy will walk across the Tallulah Gorge on a steel cable two inches in diameter," said the voice from the loudspeaker. "The length of the cable is nine hundred and eighty feet between the tower on the north side of the Gorge and the tower on this, the south side. The supporting guy wires for the cables are placed at thirty-foot intervals and are anchored in concrete at various spots down in the Gorge itself. There is no net, ladies and gentlemen. When I asked Stephen Andrassy if he was planning to rig a net, he said, 'It is unthinkable.'"

Julie tried not to listen, but it was impossible not to. She didn't want to know about cable and anchors and cavallettis. She wanted to know about Stephen. Was he nervous? Worried? Had he slept well last night? Was he ready both mentally and physically to go on the wire? And did he think of her now, at all? Because she knew that for safety's sake he must not think of her or anything else once he was on the wire.

Her stomach swam with fear, and she had developed a splitting headache right between her eyes. When the nausea threatened to become even worse, she saw a sudden flash of white satin on the other side of the Gorge, and then she spied Stephen's fluttering scarlet-lined cape. He was there! He was about to begin.

The announcer's monologue reached a feverish pitch. The crowd stirred restlessly. Julie removed the binoculars from her eyes long enough to see one woman below the observation deck cover her face with her hands. *I wish I could do that,* Julie thought to herself, and then she chided herself for even thinking it. No one had forced her to come here. She had come of her own free will. She could have chosen not to watch—and earlier, she hadn't wanted to—but now that she was here, she must not think such negative thoughts.

She raised the binoculars again and on the other side of the wide chasm she saw Stephen step onto the platform. He raised his arms, first one, then the other, in a graceful acknowledgment of the crowd's applause. He was smiling and self-assured. The wind was strong enough to ruffle his hair and he tossed his head back, so that his hair realigned itself in artful layers. Julie remembered the day the two of them had gone together for haircuts. It was the first time she remembered responding to Stephen's strong masculinity, the first time she had related to him as an interested woman relates to an attractive man. Somehow, that day seemed very long ago.

Stephen accepted his balancing pole from Albert and hefted it in his hands. Albert removed Stephen's cape with a showmanlike flourish, and Stephen stepped forward, ready to place his foot on the cable. A hush fell over the crowd.

Julie's fingers clung damply to the silvery metal of the binoculars, and she, along with everyone else, held her breath. Stephen was so majestic standing at the edge of the Gorge; he was so *beautiful*. He was so beautiful that she wanted to cry.

Not a sound could be heard in the crowd. Stephen stood erect and smiling, gathering his concentration. And then, supremely confident, he stepped out on the wire.

One foot was placed precisely and brilliantly, and then the other foot, as he slid forward in the graceful gait of the wire walker. His hips were straight and did not shift from side to side; neither did his shoulders. It was important to find balance before those first few steps, and Stephen had. He moved swiftly and gracefully, holding his balancing pole in his hands palms up. His face was calm, controlled. His whole body was calm and controlled. He had centered down in himself, and nothing intruded.

Julie barely breathed. She scarcely thought of that terrible night in New Orleans eight years ago. All she thought about was Stephen, and even though her palms were sweaty and her stomach churned, she felt a surprising elation. She concentrated so intensely on Stephen, on his every movement, that she thought she could feel the stiff breeze that blew through the Gorge. She bent with the wind, becoming a part of it, compensating for it, and she felt the wire between her big toe and her second toe, the way Stephen was feeling it now.

The balancing pole swayed slightly, caught by the wind, and Julie knew Stephen's struggle to maintain his balance, knew it intimately. For she had fought the same fight, the fight against gravity, and she knew the battle well. Move your balancing pole side to side; never sway it up and down. That was the way. That was the way to make gravity your ally, not your enemy.

Slide each foot forward surely, and don't let the wire know you are afraid. If the wire knows you are afraid, you have lost your chance to master it. And you must master the wire or die.

Be economical of movement, and don't waste any gesture. Do not, under any circumstances, break rhythm. You must not look down. You must not look at the walls of the Gorge for fear of being fooled by their illusion. You must be aware of grease drawn out of the cable by the hot sun. And you must never let thoughts intrude when you are on the wire. You must be a well-tuned machine—a machine programmed to walk the wire without fear.

Julie read the expression on Stephen's face. It was a look of the utmost concentration. He walked on, his mastery of his art evident in every studied movement. He walked on, impervious to the wind in his face. He walked on, bravely defying gravity.

"Stephen Andrassy," the announcer said in a hushed voice. "The third man to walk the wild and lovely Tallulah Gorge. There is no net, ladies and gentlemen. Stephen Andrassy walks a two-inch steel cable nine hundred and eighty feet above the Tallulah River. Below him lie sharp rocks, trees, and nine hundred and eighty feet of nothing." The announcer paused dramatically. "Remember that...as you watch...this man walk...high above the Tallulah Gorge."

Anxiety gnawed at the pit of Julie's stomach, but she didn't stop watching Stephen. She kept the binoculars trained upon him. He was, after all, the reason she was here.

The crossing was going well, Julie knew. She could tell by the exuberance on Stephen's features. He was also certain to be feeling some fatigue by now. She knew he would know how to deal with it.

Someone in the crowd gasped as Stephen stopped on the wire.

"Oh, my god," a woman cried.

"What's happening? Why is he doing that?" A well-dressed matron on the observation platform grabbed at her escort's arm.

"Now Stephen Andrassy stops," intoned the announcer, sounding puzzled. "And he—why, he's sitting *down* on the wire! Now he's—why, he appears to be *lying down*!"

Julie bit at the inside of her cheek. She was not as worried as others in the crowd. As Stephen bent one knee and slid that leg forward, his head eased back until it touched the cable. His other leg fell of the wire and dangled in space. He held his balancing pole with only one hand.

Stephen was resting during his one-thousand-foot trek across the Gorge.

Others caught on to what Stephen was doing. A ripple of amazement ran through the crowd. The announcer said, his voice jovial, "Well, would you believe that, ladies and gentlemen! Stephen Andrassy is taking a little snooze!" He laughed heartily.

Julie knew what Stephen was doing, and it wasn't snoozing. He was recentering himself, finding that point of calm and concentration before he resumed his walk. Even on the wire, he had trained all his muscles to relax when he gave them a mental command. He would be reinvigorated when he rose from the wire.

After several minutes, Stephen carefully sat up and rose slowly to his feet. The crowd went wild.

Step-by-step, Stephen progressed toward the south side of the Gorge. Step-by-step, he moved closer to safety. And he moved closer to Julie.

At the midpoint of his journey, Stephen stopped and lifted one foot to knee height. He also lifted the opposite arm in a salute to his audience. Again the crowd cheered, solidly behind him. They wanted him to succeed with this walk; they were agog with admiration for the man who would dare it.

Stephen measured his footsteps carefully, weighing the distance to the platform that he must reach. He began to control his breathing visibly, inhaling through his nose and exhaling through his mouth. Julie watched him through her binoculars, unconsciously timing her breathing to match his.

Now Stephen was in the final stage of his walk, and Julie's tension was almost unbearable. Each time Stephen's foot moved forward, she willed it to find the right place on the wire. She studied each movement, knowing that she would sense immediately if something began to go wrong. She would be able to spot the slight tensing of the wrong muscles or the sudden flicker of knowledge in Stephen's expression. With him, she tested the void. With him, she walked every inch. With him, she savored the heady sense of accomplishment.

The strain showed in his face, and the tendons in his neck stood out in relief. But he kept on, invincible. His eyes were steady and his feet were sure, and he had almost reached the south side of the Gorge.

It was only twenty feet, then ten, then five. The crowd's attention was utterly on Stephen. And then, triumphantly, he had reached the platform! Stephen Andrassy had successfully walked the Tallulah Gorge!

Every one of the Andrassy women on the observation platform was crying, including Julie. Tears ran down her face, but they were tears of relief and pride. Her heart swelled with pride at Stephen's accomplishment.

At that moment, when she and Eva and Susan caught each other in a big embrace, Julie felt bonded to her family again by a tremendous, indescribably emotional surge. Julie had willingly banished herself from the family spotlight, and now she was sharing it. For once she felt united with the rest of the Andrassys. She no longer felt left out of something exclusive and special.

On the other side of the viewing area, Stephen was jumping down from his platform, surrounded by television cameras and well-wishers.

"Let's go," Eva said, and she and Julie and Susan led the family, running.

He saw them pushing through the crowd below him, and he said in a commanding voice, "It is my family; please let them through." The crowd parted, and they rushed toward him.

But it was Julie upon whom his eyes fastened first, Julie who was the recipient of his exultant smile. And it was Julie who threw her arms around him, crying, "Stephen, oh, Stephen, it was wonderful!" She gloried in the brush of his windblown yellow hair across her cheek.

"You came to watch! Oh, Juliana, I did not dream you would!" But these words were only for her, murmured softly into her ear.

As they reluctantly broke apart, Stephen was engulfed by the others, and all too soon he was torn from them by eager photographers who wished to record Stephen standing victorious at the brink of the Gorge.

As Stephen was borne away, Julie clasped her hands beneath her chin and closed her eyes to give thanks for Stephen's triumphant crossing. And when she opened them, Eva was staring at her in a new and curious way, as though she didn't know Julie at all.

"SO WHEN ARE YOU going to tell me what's going on between you and Stephen?" Eva asked, unable to contain her interest. To Eva's delight, Julie blushed. They were driving in Julie's car along the highway toward the mountainside house where they were all going to stay overnight.

"Something is going on, then. I was right!" Eva laughed, pleased with herself.

"Nothing is going on," Julie said unconvincingly.

"Right under our noses—the two of you managed to fall in love right under our noses!"

"Eva—"

"Don't deny it, Julie. I saw the expression in his eyes after the crossing. He looked as though he wanted to devour you right on the spot."

"I—" and Julie stopped. Eva looked over to see that her cousin's eyes were brimming with tears.

"Hey, I didn't mean to upset you! Anyway, Julie, you're driving. If you're going to cry, you'd better turn the car over to me."

Julie blinked the tears away and accepted a rumpled Kleenex.

"I can't love a man who walks the wire for a living," she said after a while. "Surely you can see that."

"Oh," Eva said. "I guess I understand, sort of. With this phobia you have about the wire, it makes sense."

"You used to hate the high wire, Eva," Julie said. "I thought you would know how I feel, if anyone would."

"Well, I got over it. I'm happy as a lark up there these days. I wish you'd get over it, too."

Julie shook her head. "I've tried. I just can't." She sighed unhappily.

"Maybe you haven't tried hard enough. After all, you didn't even fall. The rest of us did."

Julie's tone was low and emphatic. "That was the worst part of all. That I wasn't on the wire with the rest of you that night."

"Is that what bugs you? Guilt?"

"Eva, you don't know, you can't possibly know—"

"Turn here," Eva interrupted, and Julie swerved her car into a road twisting up the side of a mountain. Driving required all her concentration, for which Julie was thankful. It helped her regain her composure.

She pulled her car to a stop beside several other vehicles in front of a modernistic wood house cantilevered off the side of the mountain. She let out a deep breath and yanked on the emergency brake.

"You're not angry with me for asking about you and Stephen, are you?" Eva asked anxiously.

Julie smiled a sad smile before she stepped out of the car.

"No, Eva, I'm not angry with you," she said before she hurried inside.

But Julie didn't want to admit publicly what she couldn't even face in private yet. She didn't want Eva to know that she loved Stephen Andrassy.

IT WAS LATE that night before Julie saw Stephen alone. First he had signed autographs at Tallulah Point for an hour, and then he had been interviewed by several journalists. When he arrived at the house on the mountain, he had been enveloped by the family. After eating a sumptuous catered meal provided by the producer of *Thrills!*, they had all settled down in the big circular living area to watch a special segment on the TV news magazine *Focus* about Stephen's crossing of the Gorge, his defection from the Soviet Union and the family's past performances. The program had, much to Julie's shock, touched briefly on the fall in the Superdome eight years ago.

Julie had not run from the room, even though she was fully aware that everyone expected her to do just that. Instead, she forced herself to remain seated, shaken to the core, as each succeeding image on the television screen tore at her heart. There were the Amazing Andrassys, performing the famous nine-person pyramid that night in New Orleans, their feat forever frozen on film by a news photographer who happened to be in the audience. After that came a close-up of Grandfather Anton's face reflecting his certain knowledge of something gone awry on the wire, then a picture of them tumbling through the air, all of them, the picture that had been engraved upon Julie's conscience ever since that long-ago night.

But Julie watched the whole program, even though she had never felt more wretched in her life. She even managed to sit through Stephen's short speech at the end of it.

"The Amazing Andrassys have come a long way," he said solemnly, "since that night in New Orleans. Today began a new era in family history—and soon the Amazing Andrassys will walk together again on the high wire."

Everyone clapped and cheered except Julie. But she found herself feeling decidedly confused. She hated the idea of her family's performing on the high wire. But she was proud of Stephen for completing his crossing of the Tallulah Gorge. She never thought of the night of the fall in New Orleans without considerable gut-wrenching guilt, but she had sat through a television program tonight, with its terrible pictures of the fall, and she hadn't wanted to run away. And today she had felt a wonderful sense of belonging and sharing with her family. She was, she thought with wonder, beginning to face her family's tragedy for the first time since the accident.

Eva said, "I'm turning in. I'm exhausted." Her words were punctuated by a wide yawn.

The others followed, disbanding to various wings of the house that radiated out from the hub of the living area like spokes of a huge wheel. Julie heard Tonia whining, "I don't want to go to bed, Mommy," and Nonna shushed her, offering to put Tonia to bed herself. Doors opened and closed, and Susan said, "Julie can share a room with you, Eva. I'll sleep in Nonna's room."

Someone laughed, and Julie began to turn off all the lights in the living area. Stephen, who had been standing beside a window, said suddenly, "Juliana, come look at this. It is very beautiful."

She paused and then walked slowly across the darkened room to the window. He turned, smiling, and held out his hand, pulling her close to him.

"Look," he said, holding aside the drapery.

A full moon poured silver light over the wooden deck and the trees beyond; below in a valley nestled a town, its lights glowing gold and jade and garnet and sapphire against the brilliance of the sky.

"Will you come outside with me?" he asked suddenly, and Julie knew intuitively that Stephen meant to draw the threads of their relationship tighter. She didn't object; she couldn't. She had faced her family's tragedy tonight without flinching, and there were other things she must face, too. Stephen's love for her, for one thing. Her love for him, for another.

She followed him outside into the profound silence of the night, closing the door quietly behind her. Soft mountain breezes swayed the leaves above them, and the house shimmered like quicksilver with reflected moonlight.

"I am glad you came today, Juliana," Stephen said earnestly, taking both her hands in his.

"I couldn't stay away," she murmured.

"When I saw you there, I thought it was a dream. I thought that the altitude had affected my senses." His lips curled upward in a smile.

"The farmhouse seemed so empty without everyone in it. I thought about you on the wire, and I ran and got in my car. I had to be there, with you." She shrugged lightly. "I'm glad I came. You were magnificent, Stephen. It was a masterful performance."

"The best part of it was the end, when I saw you," he said. The pleasure in his eyes was replaced by something more serious, and then, no surprise to her, he was gathering her into his arms, pressing her face into his shoulder, and stroking her long, loose hair.

She held on to him for dear life, as though she had never held him before and would never hold him again. She closed her eyes and listened to the trilling in her blood.

"You feel as I do, I can sense it," Stephen whispered against her hair.

She was conscious of her breasts pressing into his chest, and her knees felt so weak that she feared that her legs wouldn't support her. She hid her face against his neck and listened to his pulse throbbing against her cheek. She dared not speak.

Stephen's hands traced the line of her backbone, their tingling heat seeping through her thin shirt. They cupped her shoulders briefly, then held her away from him. His eyes were serious, and a question burned there. But the question faded into quiet relief when he saw the mute answer in her eyes.

He buried his face in her hair. "Tell me, Juliana. Say the words. I see it in your eyes, but I have to hear it, too." His voice was unsteady with overwhelming emotion.

"I love you, Stephen," Julie whispered. "I love you." She had thought she would never tell him, and now she wondered if she were crazy for doing it. But, oh, she did love him; she loved him with all her heart.

Stephen's arms clasped her even tighter, as though he would never let her go. Her admission of her love for him had caused her so much anguish that he felt it coursing through her body, making her muscles tense, drawing her away from him. She had finally admitted her love for him, and now he was the custodian of that love, and he was determined to care for it well.

"I love you, too, Juliana. And you will never be sorry that you love me." Softly he caressed the tender spot at the nape of her neck; slowly he felt her relax against him.

They loved each other. And now that they had established this truth, everything else would fall into place. If he trod carefully, if he kept his eye on the goal, if he proceeded with utter confidence, he could make Juliana see that a life together was the only thing that mattered.

Such a task was not, Stephen reflected, unlike walking a tightrope.

Chapter Eleven

There was no need to discuss it. They knew each other's minds as well as they knew each other's hearts. On this night, they would be together.

"Juliana—are you sure?" Stephen asked her when they were in his room, the door shut between them and the rest of the family. His hands massaged her upper arms gently.

"Yes," she whispered. "I'm sure."

"What about Eva? Aren't you roommates?"

"Eva is probably asleep," Julie said. "She won't miss me."

"The others?"

"No one will know, Stephen, unless we want them to know."

He accepted this. "I would like them to know," he said slowly. "I would like them to know that you will be my wife."

"I can't promise that," Julie said. "You know I can't promise that."

"Ah, then we must cherish this night all the more," he said, drawing her close. "It must be special."

"It already is," she said.

He noticed the tightness in her voice. "Are you nervous?" he asked. "Or worried?" His eyes shone with tender concern.

"No, not worried. Maybe a little nervous." There was no point in lying to him; he'd know.

"Don't be nervous," he said. "There is no need."

His hands caressed her shoulders, and her arms went around him, her fingers splaying over his smoothly muscled back. She let her head fall slowly backward, exposing her throat to his kisses, and he pressed his lips there, all tenderness.

His hands drifted down to cup her firm buttocks, pressing her close. She arched her body into his, amazed at the way their bodies melded together so easily. One of his hands slid upward and cupped her head, guiding her lips toward his. Lazily, drowsy with the slow sureness of it, she fitted her lips upon his. His embrace tightened as his kiss deepened, and she opened her mouth to his in joyous acceptance.

Heat rose in them, slow, hot waves of aching intensity. The heat ignited a flaming desire in both of them, a throbbing awareness that blotted out everything but the two of them, touching, kissing, wanting.

And then it was uncontrollable, a desperate seeking of two bodies that had long desired each other. Julie lost herself in his kisses, in his fervent caresses, floating away on a tide of sensation and emotion. When she thought she could no longer stand, he swept her into his arms and strode to the bed with her, gazing at her steadily and with barely muted passion for a moment before laying her carefully on top of the turned-back sheets.

"Where are you going?" she asked tremulously as he walked quickly across the room to the window.

He yanked the draperies open, revealing a panoramic view of the jewel-lit valley below.

He hurried back to the bed and stood over her, slowly unbuttoning his shirt.

"I have dreamed of you in my bed, with your hair fanned out on my pillow. Tonight, Juliana, we will have moonlight so that I can see you the way I have always dreamed of you." His shirt slid to the floor, and he reached out and turned off the light.

When her eyes adjusted to the silvery dimness, she saw that he had removed his jeans and stood above her like a moonlit statue. The planes of his face were shadowed, and the taut muscles of his torso were delineated by the brilliant light streaming in the window. Her heart swelled with love for him.

She sat up and reached her arms out to him. If she had been nervous earlier, she was not now. If she had been afraid, now she was not. Stephen was her love, the only true love she had ever had, and she had waited for him so long.

"Come to bed," she whispered softly. "Come to bed, Stephen, my love."

AFTERWARD, when they lay together in peaceful intimacy, her hair spread out across his chest, his arm cradling her securely against him, it seemed that they had always been this way. In Stephen's experience, there had never been such total sharing with a woman. He was warmed and heartened by their love for each other. He was made glad.

But he had to think of the future. Julie was scheduled to leave the farm soon. And this time she would really leave. This time there would be no reprieve.

Julie had her own thoughts. She loved him. Overriding everything else was that one fact: she loved Stephen Andrassy. What in the world was she going to do about it?

He knew when he saw her eyes were open and staring into the darkness that she was no longer lying quiescently. Something was on her mind. He wasn't sure if he should ask her about it or if he should ignore it. But how could he ignore it? Their problems wouldn't go away. They wouldn't go away unless they made them go away.

"Thinking such serious thoughts, my Juliana?" he said, tipping the edge of one finger across her bottom lip. He was rewarded when her lips curved into a smile.

"Yes," she admitted, sliding one leg between his. She thought she would never get enough of the silky feeling of warm skin against warm skin.

"Do you wish to talk about them?" he asked gently.

"Mmm," she said, undecided. In the aftermath of their lovemaking, when they were feeling so close and warm, she thought she could tell Stephen anything.

"Does that mean yes or no?" he asked.

She tightened her arm across his chest. His chest was covered with downy blond hair; it reminded her of the feathers on a baby chick. She nestled her face in it and brushed his chest with her lips.

"How was it for you today at the Gorge?" he asked. "Were you so scared for me?"

"Not—not overly so, I suppose. A few months ago I never could have imagined putting myself through it. But today I watched."

"And how do you think this happened, this change in you?"

"Love made it happen," she said slowly. "Love."

"Your love for me."

"Yes."

He slid out from under her and propped himself up on one elbow. In the moonlight, she saw that his expression was earnest.

"Do you love me enough, Juliana, to make your peace with what I do for a living?"

She stared up at him, her heartbeat escalating. She loved him so much, never more than now, but he was asking a lot.

"I don't know," she said brokenly. "I just don't know."

"If you have an anxiety attack every time I go on the wire, it is no good. I could not concentrate, knowing that you were upset."

She stared at the crease in his upper lip. It was such a sensual upper lip. But it wasn't sensual enough to distract her from the conversation.

"I know," she said.

"Your worry stems from that night of the fall in the Superdome," he said carefully, afraid to press her too hard.

"I don't want to talk about it," she said, turning away from him, her panicky feeling overridden by a sense of inevitability.

He rested a gentle hand on her shoulder. "It might be best," he said.

"No!"

"Sh, you will wake someone. All right, we will not talk of it. We will—" He broke off in mid-sentence when he realized that Julie's shoulders were shaking with sobs.

He regretted mentioning the Superdome now; he wished he had not spoken. But there was so little time!

At this point there was nothing to do but take her gently by the hip and shoulder and to turn her until she faced him, and then to enclose her in his arms and kiss away her tears.

"Hush, Juliana, it's all right. You are safe in my arms, and we will not talk about that night in New Orleans. We will never talk about it if you don't want to."

To his surprise, she struggled to break free of his embrace. She was strong and impassioned and she was breathing heavily.

He let her go, feeling hollow inside. He had ruined everything; tonight they'd had it all, and he'd ruined it by urging her to talk about the accident when she wasn't ready.

But again she surprised him. "Stephen," she said, visibly struggling to control her voice, "I will tell you what happened that night. I've never told a living soul." She paused to brush tears from her eyes, and her face took on a hard, determined look. On this soft summer night, her eyes were as bleak and as cold as a winter's day. Suddenly, inexplicably, he was frightened for her.

"No, Juliana, not if you don't want to tell me," he said, making an about-face.

She sat bolt upright, kneeling on the bed, completely naked in the relentlessly brilliant light of the moon. The sharp, clear light would illuminate any nuance of expression.

In the moonlight, her cheeks were ashen. She shook her head relentlessly, driving herself. She neither asked for nor gave herself any quarter.

"This is how it happened," Julie said, and she proceeded to tell him about that terrible night in New Orleans all those long years ago.

ON THAT FATEFUL JOURNEY, the Amazing Andrassys' time in New Orleans was limited; they had arrived late one night and had gone directly to their hotel suite. The next night, Saturday, they would perform at the Louisiana Superdome, the largest covered stadium in the world, in a special show to benefit handicapped children. They were scheduled to fly to their next engagement early Sunday morning.

On Saturday morning, while Grandfather Anton and Julie's father, Sandor, and Uncle Béla had been setting up the rigging at the Superdome, a delighted seventeen-year-old Julie had explored the antique shops on Royal Street in the French Quarter with her mother, whose name was Elisabeth, and Eva.

Julie's brother, Tony, and Paul, Michael and Albert were quickly bored with antiques and had cheerfully splintered off from the female contingent to take an eager look at Bourbon Street, well-known for its nightclubs of every description.

"You wouldn't believe the characters we saw while we were just walking on Bourbon Street," Tony had enthused afterward, when they all met back at the hotel restaurant for lunch. "There was a man who stood on the street corner playing seven instruments at one time. And we peeked in a topless bar and saw this—"

"Did you tell Julie about the sidewalk painter?" Paul interrupted hastily.

"No, that's something she'll have to see for herself," Tony said with a grin.

"Well, let's go over to Bourbon Street right now," Julie suggested, jumping up from her chair in the restaurant. "C'mon, everybody."

"No, Julie," her father said. "Everyone must rest this afternoon for the performance tonight."

"Oh, pooh," Julie said, slumping back into her chair. "Here we are in the most interesting city in the United States, and I have to sit around this hotel all afternoon." She glared daggers at her father, who ignored her.

But in the elevator on the way back to the family suite, Paul told Julie quietly, "The guys are going out after the performance tonight. We'll take in the jazz at Preservation Hall, maybe go to a few nightclubs while we're at it. You can come with us if you like."

Julie had brightened at this idea. "Thanks, Paul. I will." She shot him a happy smile as she and Eva left the group and went into the room they shared.

Eva flopped on the bed. Then, as now, Eva had required lots of sleep.

"Wake me in plenty of time to get ready for the performance," Eva told Julie as she plumped up her pillow and settled into it.

"Okay. Say, are you going with us to Bourbon Street tonight after the show?"

Eva yawned. "I doubt it. I'd rather stay here and read a book. You're not thinking of going, are you?"

"Sure. Paul invited me."

"I bet you won't go. It doesn't sound like something your parents will let you do."

"Why, I'm almost eighteen years old now. I'm practically an adult." Julie was indignant to think that her parents might think she was too young.

"You'd better check with them first," Eva cautioned, knowing how strict both her own parents and Julie's parents could be.

Before long, Eva was sound asleep. Julie wasn't really tired, so she leafed through an old copy of *Seventeen* and tried to get interested in the stories, but they all seemed too juvenile, geared to teenagers. She was a full-fledged member of a talented performing troupe, earning her own living. Stories about girls trying to get boys to talk to them in study hall just didn't satisfy her anymore.

Finally, tossing the magazine impatiently aside, Julie stood and went to the window. The city was spread out before her in all its glory—the Superdome, the French Quarter, the Mississippi River. She wished she were out there exploring it—but of course, it was Grandfather Anton's rule that they all must rest in the afternoon before a performance, and all the Andrassys rigidly observed this rule. When they were performing the nine-person pyramid, any one of the Andrassys could be the weak link that caused the pyramid to crumble. It was supremely important to be in excellent physical and mental condition before attempting it.

Julie heard quiet voices in the living room of their hotel suite. First she heard Grandfather Anton's low rumbling tones, and then her mother's higher ones. Finally her father joined in. This was perfect—a time when she could speak to them privately about going out with her brother and her older male cousins. Quietly she opened the door of their room and slipped into the living room.

Her mother saw her standing respectfully by her door, politely waiting for Grandfather Anton to finish talking.

"Why, Julie, you should be resting," her mother scolded, unwittingly starting everything off on a negative note.

"I'm not tired," Julie retorted. Her mother's scolding tone made her hackles rise.

"Please go back to your room and rest for tonight, Julie," Grandfather Anton had said. He sounded stern, but then as family patriarch he was always stern about infractions of the rules he had established.

"No," Julie said defensively, causing her father's eyebrows to lift sky high.

"Julie, you heard your Grandfather." Her father was firm. Grandfather Anton's word was law.

"What I mean is, Paul and the boys have asked me to go out with them tonight after the show. May I, Father?"

Her father wrinkled his forehead. "You have not ever gone out with them before," he said.

"They've never invited me before. And we've never been in New Orleans. Please, I want to see—more of the city." Julie had the good sense not to mention the wonders of Bourbon Street; she thought her father might object.

"Julie, you are only seventeen years old. I believe you are too young to go out with the boys." Her grandfather eyed her sternly.

"Eva goes with them sometimes."

"Eva is considerably older than you are."

"Only by a few years. Anyway, the boys get to go out all the time, wherever we're performing. You let them stay out until all hours last New Year's Eve in

New York." With typical teenage pique, Julie was determined not to be as docile as she normally was.

"It is different for boys. And they are also older than you are."

"Grandfather Anton, things have changed. Nowadays girls do whatever boys do. Anyway, my brother and my cousins aren't boys—they're men. And at eighteen, I'm hardly a girl—I'm a woman." Julie tossed her head.

"You are not eighteen yet, Julie. And in this family, things have not changed. If I say you cannot go out late at night, you cannot. I don't want to hear any more about it." Grandfather Anton turned his back. Ever the old-world autocrat, he knew how to be strict.

Desperately, Julie tried to think of a persuasive argument. But this authoritarian old man was accustomed to having his way in everything; he was the boss of the family, both on the high wire and off it.

Something in her snapped. She was sick of having to do what he said all the time, even though he thought he had her best interests at heart. She desperately wanted out from under his thumb, and she longed to make her own decisions for once. Her independence would have to come someday, and to her way of thinking, that someday was now. What better way to prove her independence once and for all than by going with the boys to Bourbon Street that night?

"I don't have to do what you say," she said in a low angry tone. "And I won't."

"Julie," her mother began, visibly distressed.

"I mean it. In a few months I'll be legally old enough to drink and old enough to vote. I'm a modern American girl, and Grandfather Anton's thinking is old-country and old-fashioned.'' She stuck out her bottom lip stubbornly.

"Do not attack your grandfather, Juliana!" barked her father, who would not stand for revolt against the family patriarch from his own child.

Julie's mother advanced toward her daughter, holding out both hands in a gesture of supplication.

"After the show tonight we will go for a snack together, you and me. Would you like that, Julie?" Clearly Elisabeth was trying to spread oil on troubled waters, but Julie was not to be distracted from what she saw as a major step in her maturing process.

"No, Mother," she said defiantly. "I'm going out with the boys."

Grandfather Anton whirled and confronted her with beetle brows lowered.

"That is enough," he said.

"You are wrong, Grandfather! You see me as the baby of this troupe, but I carry a full performing load just like the others! Why won't you let me have the privileges of an adult? It isn't fair!" Dusky spots of color flared in her cheeks, but she stood her ground.

Elisabeth could never bear any dissension within the family. Quiet and soft-spoken herself, she was always the peacemaker.

"Father Anton," she said placatingly to her father-in-law, "perhaps just this once—"

"Elisabeth!" Julie's father said in shock. None of them ever questioned Grandfather Anton's benevolent dictatorship.

"But Sandor—" Elisabeth said, clearly distressed to be caught in the battle between generations.

"Enough! Julie has caused enough trouble." Sandor's dark eyes flashed the same fire as his daughter's, and he folded his lips into an unyielding line.

"Please, children, do not argue," Grandfather Anton said imperatively.

Julie took a step backward, bewildered by what she had accomplished. She had meant to get permission to go to Bourbon Street that night, and all she had managed to do was start a hair-raising family row. Now her father was insisting that her mother leave the room and let the two men handle the problem with Julie, and her mother was crying. Julie had stirred up a tempest, all right. She wished she could feel some sort of grim satisfaction about it, but all she felt was sadness.

She fled to the bedroom, where Eva was sprawled on her bed on her stomach, sound asleep. Through the closed door Julie heard her father and mother arguing. They weren't arguing loudly, but they certainly were arguing fervently. And Grandfather Anton was trying his best to smooth everything over.

Well, what would she do now? She obviously wasn't any closer to going out that night than she had been when she started. She lay on her back on her bed, wondering if she could possibly sneak out. No, that would never work. Her mother always stepped into her room to check on her, and maybe pull the covers up before she herself went to bed. Perhaps she should have taken Elisabeth up on her offer to go out for a snack after the show tonight. Maybe she could finagle her mother into checking out Bourbon Street with her.

The argument in the living room diminished, then died out altogether. Her mother and father had gone to their room, and Grandfather Anton had gone to his. He always rested before a performance like everyone else, and he always called Nonna at home during his rest period. He was probably telephoning Nonna right now.

Julie must have fallen asleep, because the next thing she knew, her brother Tony was knocking gently on her door.

"Julie! Eva! Time to go to the Superdome!"

Julie kept quiet during the ride to the arena; since no one mentioned the argument with her parents and Grandfather Anton, apparently no one else had heard it. This didn't surprise her; the bedroom that she and Eva shared was the only one that opened off the living room of their suite. The other bedrooms were situated off a long hall, and the door from the hall to the living room had been closed.

"All right," Grandfather Anton said when they had assembled in a quiet place outside their dressing rooms for costume check. They lined up, impressive in their blue leotards with the shiny silver spangles. Grandfather Anton consulted his clipboard. "Tonight are scheduled to perform—let's see—me, Sandor, Béla, Paul, Albert, Tony, Eva, Julie and Michael. Elisabeth, you will sit out tonight."

"Julie, are you coming with us tonight to Bourbon Street?" Michael said, leaning toward her and speaking in an undertone.

"No, Grandfather and my parents won't let me," Julie whispered back.

Michael opened his eyes wide. "No kidding! Why, I'm going! I thought they'd let you go if I went!"

This galled Julie particularly, because Michael was only a few months older than she. Her father, standoffish toward Julie on the way to the Superdome, caught her eye and sent her a look which unmistakably meant "be quiet!" Her mother, red-eyed as though she had been crying, stared down at the floor. Julie could tell that her mother was still miserable over the afternoon's argument.

"Now," Grandfather Anton was saying encouragingly, psyching them up for the performance as he always did. "We have a large crowd out there, and we will give them our best. Remember—no other troupe in America performs the nine-person pyramid. We are the very best on the high wire." Then he paused as he always did. What he was to say next was the most important part of his speech before a show.

"Is everyone feeling well? If there is any reason, mental or physical, why you cannot go on the wire, please tell me now." His dark eyes swept over the troupe. It was his policy that anyone could refuse to go on the wire, with no questions asked. That was why there were ten performing Andrassys and only nine in their famous pyramid.

Suddenly Julie, acting purely out of spite, stepped forward. "I cannot go on the wire, Grandfather," she said. She was aware of Eva's quick, puzzled glance. Her father's head shot up, and his eyes narrowed.

Grandfather smiled, their earlier argument forgiven. "That is fine, Julie. If you feel that you are not ready, Elisabeth will take your place. Elisabeth?"

"Yes," her mother said, reaching in front of Michael and solicitously touching the back of her hand to Julie's forehead. "I will go instead of Julie." She dropped her hand at Julie's hostile stare, looking relieved that Julie didn't have a fever.

"Julie, is something wrong?" Eva asked as the performers slipped on their wooden clogs for the walk to the arena.

"I don't feel well," Julie said, refusing to smile.

"Well, then," Eva said. But she was obviously perplexed. Julie was always in the best of health and had never sat out before when scheduled to perform.

Julie's mother reached over and gave Julie an unexpected hug. But Julie scowled and stared straight ahead. She was still angry at the three of them—her father, her mother and Grandfather Anton.

The band in the arena struck up a brassy fanfare, and the performing troupe donned their blue satin capes and lined up in order, with stately Grandfather Anton in the lead. Then, as the crowd cheered, they marched briskly in time to the music into the arena, heads held high, right arms upraised, smiling and confident. No one would guess that any of them had been involved in a family row just hours before.

Julie, alone in the corridor, almost went back to the dressing room to wait out the performance. But for some reason, she changed her mind and tugged a raincoat on over her costume. Then she slipped into the arena and sat on the sidelines, watching as the Amazing Andrassys climbed the tall ladder to the platform where they would embark upon their journey on the wire—their last journey on the wire together for a long, long time.

Chapter Twelve

For two or three minutes after Julie's low voice ceased to speak, nothing was said between the two of them. Julie, her hands clasped in front of her, stared into space, reliving the nightmare of that night. Overwhelmed by the sorrow with which she told her story, Stephen was reluctant to break the silence.

Finally he said quietly, "It must have been very difficult for you to tell me this."

She looked at him, and it was with relief that he saw that her eyes were clear and bright, not glazed with tears.

"It was," she admitted, "but I feel better for it."

"So you have been living with this self-imposed guilt all these years," he said, caressing her forearm.

"I have been living with guilt, but it wasn't exactly self-imposed. It was real, Stephen." Her eyes, black as onyx, glinted with self-loathing.

"Many things can go wrong on the wire. You were not on the wire that night with the others. There is no way you could possibly know what caused the pyramid to fall."

"I *know* what caused it to fall. It was my mother. She was the weak link that night. I saw her falter on the bar where she balanced between my father's and Michael's shoulders; I saw her desperately try to save herself. But it was too late by the time she lost her balance. And then she took all of them with her.'' Julie shuddered, remembering the panic-stricken look on her mother's face as she frantically attempted and failed to grasp a guy wire as she fell.

"This is not your fault, Juliana.'' Stephen lifted himself up from the pillows and tried to pull her close, but she shook his hands off impatiently and stared down at her interwoven fingers.

"Of course it's my fault. Stephen, don't you see? I refused to go on the wire for no reason at all except my stupid teenage tantrum, and my mother took my place. She was still upset about our argument that afternoon, but she thought I was sick! So she went up anyway! *She* is the one who should have sat out that night, not me!'' Julie spat out the words, and Stephen's chest constricted at the thought of the torture that she had hidden in her soul all these years.

"So afterward, you shouldered sole responsibility for taking care of Nonna, is that right? Because it was your fault that Grandfather Anton and the others died?''

Julie nodded, pressing one hand to her mouth as if to contain the grief knotting in her throat.

"Haven't you ever told anyone else any part of this story?''

Julie shook her head. "No. No one knew about the argument except Grandfather, Mother, Father and me. And they were dead. I couldn't bear for the others to know that I was the reason the accident happened. How could they ever forgive me?'' Her voice quavered pathetically.

Stephen was silent for a time, but then he reached out for her. Now, when he tried to pull her into his embrace, she didn't resist. He bent his head to kiss her, and her ferocity caught him off guard. This time Julie seemed to want to savage him in frenzied need, raking her fingers through his hair, heaving her body against his, pitching and clutching as though she were trying to exorcise all the dark spaces within herself. When at last they gasped in paralyzed pleasure, needing nothing more from each other, Stephen rolled away but remained linked to her by their hands.

She sighed and smiled briefly at him before she slept, but Stephen remained thoughtfully awake until the moonlight faded and dawn shimmered beyond the mountain. When he saw the encroaching light through the uncurtained window, he knew that soon he must awaken Julie so that she could creep back to the room she shared with Eva before anyone in the house awoke.

The sun wove pale streamers of light into the gray sky, and still Stephen stared at the ceiling. Beside him, Julie continued to sleep, her breathing soft and steady. He looked at her, so beautiful with her hair fanned out around her face. He loved her more than any other woman he had ever known, and he couldn't bear to think of going through life without her.

Yet the night was almost over, and nothing concrete had been settled between them; a new day had begun, and Stephen could only hope that it would be symbolic of a new beginning in his relationship with Julie.

But he was not one to depend wholly on hope. He was one to spring into action when the situation warranted it. He understood now that the time had come to do more than wait.

Stephen knew that the time had arrived for him to find a way to demolish the web of concealment and deceit that had paralyzed this family for so long. Newly armed with the information Julie had revealed, Stephen now felt prepared to fight for her and for their life together.

"THE NIGHT OF THE FALL in New Orleans?" Albert asked in consternation. "Why do you want to know about it?"

"Because I would like to know what caused the fall."

Albert shrugged and stared into his coffee cup. They had driven down from the mountain in the morning to buy a newspaper. Stephen had offered to treat Albert to breakfast, and they were sitting in a booth at a small café on the highway near the town of Tallulah Falls.

When Albert raised his eyes to Stephen's, they were hesitant. "That night on the wire," he began, and then stopped. His look was troubled.

"Go on," Stephen prompted. His curiosity was aroused. Why did Albert look so guilty?

"I've never talked about that night," Albert said in an apologetic tone.

"It's been many years since the accident, Albert," Stephen said gently. "It's all right to talk about it."

Albert was silent for a long time, but then he spoke. "Well," he said, "on the afternoon of the performance, I talked Tony—Julie's brother, who was killed—I talked him into sneaking out of our room in the hotel suite. No one was around, so we tiptoed out of our room and locked the door behind us. There was an emergency stairway right next to our suite, so getting out of the hotel without being seen was no big deal. We'd been to Bourbon Street in the morning, and we had a hankering to go back.''

"It was Grandfather Anton's rule that everyone rested the afternoon before a performance," Stephen said.

"Yes," Albert said, seeming to pull himself back from a place faraway in his thoughts. "Anyway, we went to Bourbon Street, and there was this topless bar that was open all day. Tony had gotten a glimpse inside the place when we were there that morning, and since we'd never been to any place remotely like it, we were eager to go back."

"And so you did?"

"We sure did. We went inside that topless bar, drank a couple of beers and leered at the girls. Then we ran back to the hotel, sneaked back up the emergency stairway, and let ourselves back into our locked room. But you know, Stephen, I've always wondered if—" Albert stopped and stared into his coffee cup again as though he thought it could provide an answer.

"Go on," Stephen prodded.

Albert raised haunted eyes to Stephen. As long as he had known Stephen, Albert had never known him to be unfair or judgmental. Finally, he could get his disturbing thoughts about that night off his chest.

"I've always wondered," he said slowly, "if the beers we drank that afternoon made a difference. We weren't supposed to drink anything alcoholic on the day of a performance until after the performance was over." He watched Stephen levelly for his reaction.

Stephen was shaken by Albert's revelation, but he tried not to show it. "It could have made your reaction time slower," he replied, "and if you reacted more slowly, you might not have responded to any difficulty on the wire as swiftly as you might have normally."

"That's true," Albert said. "Tony and I—we were just a couple of young studs in those days. We thought we could handle a few beers—I mean, what's a few beers? And it was hours later that we performed. But I've always felt guilty. As you know, Tony died in that fall. If only I'd said 'Hey, Tony, we'd better not sneak out of the hotel,' or if I'd insisted that we order soft drinks instead of beer at the bar."

"You should not blame yourself, Albert," Stephen said reassuringly. "Sneaking out of the hotel was a dumb thing to do, but who is to say that the fall was your fault? It could have been anyone's fault—or no one's."

"What do you mean by that?" Albert asked, looking confused.

"I'm not sure," Stephen said, with a curious sense of elation. "I'm not sure—yet."

MICHAEL, ENJOYING THIS DAY off from practice on the wire, laughed at Mickey's antics on the elaborate play equipment near the house jutting off the mountainside. The sun blazed down out of a brilliant sky, picking out the red highlights in his son's hair.

Michael was happy, a family man taking the time to enjoy his children, as Mickey and Tonia gamboled on the custom-built monkey bars and swings and slide. He was happy, so why did Stephen have to come around and pester him with questions about that night in New Orleans? Michael had tried his best to forget everything about it.

Stephen wrinkled his forehead. "Please think about it, Michael," he begged. "Think of anything unusual you can remember about that night."

Michael chewed on a long blade of grass. Stephen seemed so intense, and he did want to please Stephen. After all, Stephen was responsible for getting them all back on the high wire. If it hadn't been for Stephen, there would be no future in the family act for Mickey and Tonia, who were now, in imitation of their father and aunts and uncles, trying to outdo each other with outrageous tricks on the monkey bars.

Michael sighed. "Well, let me think. I was excited about going out that night—we were going to Bourbon Street, I remember. And I was learning to take care of the equipment we used in the act." Here Michael's face clouded.

"Something about the equipment?" Stephen prompted.

"Yes," Michael said quietly. "There was something wrong with my shoulder brace. And it was my fault."

"How?"

"Grandfather Anton asked me to check the shoulder braces while the others were in the dressing room at the Superdome getting ready for the act. He left me alone in the corridor, and you know what I did? I smoked a cigarette."

"I didn't know you smoked," Stephen said.

"I don't. But I had just turned eighteen and in those days I thought it was a grown-up thing to do. Of course, Grandfather Anton was against the use of tobacco of any kind. He expected us to train like the top-notch athletes we were, and tobacco was forbidden.''

''As well it should be,'' Stephen said.

Michael nodded in agreement. ''So I had to sneak it. I hid behind the wardrobe trunk in the corridor and smoked a cigarette. Grandfather Anton came out of the dressing room looking for me, and he asked me if the equipment was all checked out. I lied and said it was. I figured it wouldn't hurt if one time I didn't look at every brace.''

''And something was wrong with the equipment?''

''Yeah. The braces are made out of leather-padded steel, and it just didn't occur to me that anything could go wrong. But the leather strap and buckle must have been loose or something, because I felt my brace shift just a little bit, hardly enough to notice, and Aunt Elisabeth, who was balancing on the pole held between my shoulder brace and Uncle Sandor's, started to fall.'' For a moment Michael looked immeasurably sad, and then he called something to Tonia about not going down the slide backward.

''But then you have thought that the accident was your fault!'' Stephen said in astonishment.

''Yeah, I guess I have. I've tried not to think about it, but there it is.'' Michael shook his head philosophically. ''Maybe it was just the breaks of the game, you know? But I can tell you one thing—I've never smoked a cigarette since that night.'' Michael turned his attention to his children again, plainly unwilling to discuss this disquieting topic anymore.

But Stephen didn't care. He had found out more than he needed to know.

"MIND IF I KEEP YOU company?" Eva asked, knocking at the open door of Stephen's bedroom.

Stephen continued to fold his satin cape in tissue paper and placed it in its box.

"No, Eva, of course I don't mind. Please come in."

Eva sat down on the edge of the bed and picked up his buffalo-hide slippers. They were old and soft and worn. She handed them to Stephen and watched while he wrapped them, too, in paper.

"I heard Albert and Michael talking about the questions you've been asking," Eva said hesitantly. She turned troubled eyes upon Stephen.

"Oh?" he said, lifting his eyebrows.

"I—I thought if you wanted me to tell you anything about that night, I would be glad to discuss it."

Actually, Stephen had not been planning to ask Eva. Albert and Michael had provided him with enough information for his purposes. But he stopped folding his costume and said softly, "What do you remember about that night, Eva?"

Eva shook her short hair back from her face and inspected her fingernails for a long moment. Then she took a deep breath.

"I remember how unhappy I was that I was away from my boyfriend that night."

"You had a boyfriend?"

"His name was Clark, and he was the first man I ever loved. That day of the accident was his twenty-first birthday, and his parents were giving a big birthday party for him at their country club, but I couldn't go because I had to perform with the act!"

"And so you sulked."

"Yes, I sulked the whole trip."

"And you were angry on the wire that night?"

"I wasn't exactly angry up there on the wire. But I was having a hard time getting Clark out of my head, and that's no good, you know. You should clear everything from your mind when you're up there on that cable—but why am I telling you this? You already know it." The line of her lips was grim.

"And let me guess—all this time you have blamed yourself for the fall?"

"When Aunt Elisabeth started to lose her balance, I should have been alert enough to notice. We were both on the top tier of the pyramid, and if I hadn't been thinking about Clark and his birthday party, if I had kept my mind on business like I should have, I might have been able to counterbalance Aunt Elisabeth so that it might not have happened."

"You think that made a difference on the night of the fall? You think your personal feelings contributed to it?"

"I'm sure of it!"

"Would it help if I told you that there was probably nothing you could have done when Elisabeth faltered?"

Eva smiled a sad little smile. "No, not much."

"That is what I thought," Stephen said, and understandingly, he clasped her shoulder for a moment.

"What difference does it make?" Eva asked. "I mean, why do you want to know about that night?"

Stephen removed his hand from her shoulder and stood thinking for a moment. He appeared to be weighing something in his mind, and Eva watched him, wondering what was wrong.

"I think," Stephen said, closing the box where he had packed his costume, "that it is time to have a talk.

You, Eva, and Albert and Michael and Paul. And Julie.''

"Not about the fall," Eva said, shaking her head in denial. She never liked to think about the fall.

"Yes, about the fall," Stephen replied firmly. "For too long this family has avoided the subject. Will you help me gather them together?"

They met in the big circular living area. Eva sat on the edge of the couch; a bewildered Julie, summarily called away from counting out Nonna's pill dosage, perched beside her. Albert sat down in front of the big round fireplace in the center of the room, and Michael stood uneasily next to a window. Paul sat in a chair opposite the couch, leaning over and resting his elbows on his knees. He looked up at Stephen questioningly.

"What's up, Stephen?" he asked.

Stephen, with a reassuring look at Julie, walked to the center of the room, where he stood and looked contemplatively around the family circle.

Julie didn't understand why she had been requested to be there. She didn't understand it, but somehow she knew that this conference concerned her. She moistened her lips and darted her eyes from one cousin to the other, searching for clues.

"It has now been more than two months since we began rehearsing for the Amazing Andrassys to return to the high wire," Stephen said. "In that time we have learned many things, and we have come to know each other in ways we never did before."

Michael lifted his head and smiled. In the past two months, he had become friends with his brothers, sister and cousin. He had never felt that any of them were his friends before.

Stephen continued. "I told Julie when we arrived at the farm that a cable in the air connects two points in space. If I walk the cable, I am the connector. I am the person who makes those two points in space one."

Albert lifted his eyebrows. Julie suspected that Albert wondered where these words were leading. For that matter, so did she. Nervously she returned her attention to Stephen.

"I believed at that time that there were spaces to be connected between members of the Andrassy family. I wanted the family to be as close as it was in the old days, before the accident in New Orleans. I knew that once the Andrassy family again performed on the high wire, you would no longer be apart in loneliness. No more would we be scattered, with Albert in Mexico, Michael in Texas and Eva in Florida."

How could Julie have forgotten the impassioned case Stephen had made for going back on the wire that first day on the farm when she had gone down to the meadow and helped him to check the cable for meat hooks? And now he was looking equally as intense. But where was he leading them?

"If we are to work together in harmony on the wire, there cannot be any grudges or secrets held over from the old days. It is time for me connect those spaces—those dark spaces—you have all hidden in your minds. I am talking about the accident." His serious blue eyes scanned their faces. Julie felt the blood rush from her head, but the expression on Stephen's face said, "trust me."

But, oh, what was he doing? She thought about the night before, when she had sat on his bed and told him everything. She had emptied herself to him in confidence. Was Stephen planning to betray that confidence?

"Stephen," she began, her heart twisting in pain. She didn't want him to say what he had gathered them together to hear, and she felt her skin grow clammy with fear.

"No, Juliana, let me finish," he said purposefully, and she thought in that moment how Stephen was truly the head of the Amazing Andrassys troupe now. The way all of them looked to Stephen for guidance reminded her of the way they had all looked to Grandfather Anton in the old days. But there was a difference in style between Grandfather Anton and Stephen. Their family unity now was more democratic, with Stephen the acknowledged leader rather than a self-appointed one. And he was more than their leader. He was as he had wished to be—the heart and the soul of the Andrassy troupe.

"You have not spoken of the accident much among yourselves," Stephen went on. "We are not here to cry over our loved ones who were lost that night, but to enlighten the living. For too long the experience of the accident has been clouded by doubt and shrouded in secrecy, with each of you thinking that you and you alone were to blame for the accident."

Julie gasped. The rest of them looked nonplussed. Julie stood and would have bolted from the room if Stephen had not swiftly crossed the room and slid a supportive arm around her shoulders.

"Please sit down, Juliana," he said softly. She didn't know if she obeyed because he told her to or if her legs simply wouldn't support her, but Julie sank back onto the couch next to Eva, who reached out and took her hand.

Paul looked uncomfortable. "Stephen, are you sure about this? I'm not convinced that we need to put ourselves through it."

Paul was the one person in the room with whom Stephen hadn't spoken about that fatal night. Stephen suddenly wished he had. Maybe Paul would be the person to start. He was older than the others, and since he wasn't planning to perform on the wire again, he had less at stake.

"Paul, the others have shared their memories of that day and night with me. Do you have any recollections about what happened—and why it happened?"

Paul reflected silently for a moment, staring down at the sand-colored carpet.

"Aunt Elisabeth was upset," he said at last. "And she was upset at me."

Julie felt the onset of panic. Everything that she told Stephen last night in privacy was going to be revealed! Why, why had she told him?

"Upset at *you*?" Stephen said with a sidelong look at Julie to see how she was taking this. She wasn't taking it well; she looked pale and drawn.

"Yes, Aunt Elisabeth had seen me whispering to Julie as we walked down the hall toward our suite after lunch, and she guessed correctly that I was the one who had invited Julie to come with me and the guys to Bourbon Street that night. She—"

"You *knew*?" cried Julie. "You knew we argued?" She couldn't believe that the secret she had kept for so many years wasn't a secret at all.

"Only because Aunt Elisabeth told me. She was angry with me for not knowing better than to invite you to go with us. You were just a kid, she said, and I shouldn't have encouraged you to think you could go out with the guys. She was right. I knew how strict our parents and Grandfather Anton were. Well, before we all assembled outside the dressing room, I was in the corridor getting our capes out of the wardrobe trunk and Aunt Elisabeth came marching up and really lit into me. She said that as the oldest of the cousins, I had a certain responsibility where the younger members of the troupe were concerned, and that under no circumstances was I to pull such a stunt again.'' Paul shook his head sorrowfully. Then he looked Julie right in the eye. ''That's what happened. Aunt Elisabeth wasn't mentally prepared to go on the wire that night. And it was my fault.''

''Yours!'' Julie said, crying out as though someone had just slipped a knife into her heart. ''No, Paul! It was my fault! I had a terrible fight with Mother and Father and Grandfather Anton while the rest of you were resting that afternoon. It started over going out with the boys that night, but it became much more than that. I was angry because I had to work as a member of the troupe, but they never let me have adult privileges. Mother and Father ended up yelling at each other, and Grandfather tried to smooth everything over. Then, knowing that my mother was upset over the argument, I said I wanted to sit out during the performance. Mother took my place on the wire only because she thought I might be sick. Paul, the accident wasn't *your* fault!''

''But that's ridiculous!'' Michael interrupted. ''I've always known why the accident happened! It was because the shoulder brace I wore slipped, and Aunt Elisabeth had to struggle to keep her balance! That's why the accident happened.''

Everyone started to talk at once. Stephen attempted to calm them, but Albert said hotly, "I wasn't aware of any of those things! What I remember is that Tony and I defied Grandfather's orders by sneaking down to Bourbon Street where we drank two beers apiece. And that was the reason—"

"Will all of you be quiet!" Eva screamed, clearly beside herself. "We fell because I was thinking about Clark Fedderman and his birthday party at his parents' club, and I couldn't be there because of the trip to New Orleans, and Aunt Elisabeth slipped and I didn't react in time; there wasn't anything I could do, not a thing, and, oh, I'm so sorry!" Eva burst into tears, and Julie, shocked by what had been revealed here, clasped Eva in her arms as tears streamed down her own colorless face.

Suddenly the room was quiet except for Eva's soft, muffled sobs.

"You see?" Stephen said, his eyes circling the stunned group. "It is foolish to go on blaming yourselves. It was an accident. Maybe it was everyone's fault, or maybe it was no one's fault. It makes no difference now."

Eva stopped sobbing, and Julie reached up a trembling hand to wipe the tears from her own cheeks.

"What Stephen says it true," Albert said slowly, recovering his composure. "We have all denied our memories of the accident for much too long. And now that we're united as a family, it doesn't hurt so much to remember it. Now that we *have* remembered it, maybe we're all ready to forgive ourselves."

"I agree," said Michael, who was deeply shaken.

Paul said thoughtfully, "It is time to know that whatever happened that night, we must all stop hating ourselves. We are a family. If you hate yourself, you are hating one of us. And to hate one of us is to hate us all.''

"I don't like this talk of hating," Julie said. "We must love one another. That's why we have one another, isn't it? To love?"

Stephen walked slowly to her side, and she lifted her eyes to his. Her features had relaxed, and she looked more beautiful than he had ever seen her. His eyes bored into hers.

"Yes, Juliana," he said gently. "That is why we have one another. To love." And he bent down and kissed her on the cheek.

Chapter Thirteen

The air on this late August day seemed lit with sunshine, and Julie, on her way back to the farmhouse from the mailbox at the road, stuffed the few envelopes in the back pocket of her shorts and ran through the meadow toward the brook. The Andrassy family had arrived back at the farm two weeks ago, and she and Nonna were leaving the next day for home. Julie wanted to bid a quick farewell to the brook where she and Stephen had first had a serious conversation. It was, more than any other place, the place where they had begun to reach out to each other.

The glade beside the stream was shadowed and quiet, and she was surprised when a figure detached itself from the rocks and strode toward her, resplendent in white shorts and shirt against a deep tan. Stephen caught her in his arms and kissed her on the mouth.

She laughed up at him. "There's no telling where you'll turn up!" she teased. "How did you know I would be here?"

"I did not know you would be here, but I would have made sure you got here eventually," Stephen said. "And I will keep 'turning up,' as you so charmingly put it, the rest of your life, if you will let me."

Her expression darkened as she pulled away. "Not now, Stephen," she said. "I want to remember our last day here as a day of happiness."

He dropped a kiss on the side of her neck and led her to the flat rock where they had sat on their first night here.

"So do I. This should be a day to live in our memories, and we should have time to ourselves. That is why I have brought our lunch," he said, indicating a basket.

"Stephen!" She was touched.

"You are not to do a thing. You must sit down and let me take care of this." Julie sat, and he knelt beside her, energetically beginning to remove things from the basket and setting them on a linen tablecloth that he had spread out on the rock.

Julie leaned back on her hands, let her head fall back, and gazed up at the feathery branches overhead. The air was redolent with the scent of green moss, and the creek water glittered and gurgled between flat brown rocks. When she looked at Stephen, his face was spangled with green-and-gold light.

"I hope you like strawberries," he said, setting them out in a glass bowl.

"Why, yes," she replied in surprise. She loved strawberries.

"There I was in the grocery store buying the food for this picnic, and I had to stop and think, 'Does Juliana like strawberries?' I have so many things to learn about you." He smiled at her and produced two stemmed crystal glasses from the basket. A champagne bottle followed, and Stephen secured it between two rocks in the stream, "to chill it even more," he said.

"You've thought of everything," she marveled when she saw the curried chicken salad delectably served in hollowed brioches. "Surely you didn't do all this yourself?"

"But of course I did. You see? You have much to learn about me, too." Stephen grinned at her and dipped a strawberry in powdered sugar. "Open your mouth," he commanded, and when she did, he popped the strawberry into it.

Julie's teeth bit down on the strawberry and the juice ran down her chin. Stephen, his eyes suddenly soulful, bent over and kissed away the dribble of juice, then aligned his lips properly with hers and drew her into a deep and hungry kiss. Her hands knotted into fists on the rock, and, fighting for balance, she lifted her quivering arms to encircle his neck.

"This is very nice," he murmured lazily in her ear. "But will you look at what is happening to our champagne?"

The bottle had dislodged from its place between the rocks and was threatening to float downstream. Stephen grabbed at it wildly and slid sideways until he was half in, half out of the water. Julie instinctively reached for him, lost her balance and tumbled past him to land right side up in the shallow stream, its pebbles smooth against her legs.

She laughed up at Stephen, whose shock of fair straight hair shimmered in the mist of spray she had sent flying.

"Care to join me?" she asked jokingly, holding out her hand. She was completely surprised when he let go of the rock on which he had a firm grip and slid down it into the water beside her.

At her startled look, he only laughed. "I was already half in anyway," he offered in explanation.

"And it's a hot day," she said, because the water felt good against her skin. Then she giggled at the idea of the two of them, sitting waist deep in clear water and carrying on a perfectly normal conversation.

"If the water were deep enough, I would like to swim," Stephen said, lounging backward.

"We could wade," Julie suggested, watching minnows dart past Stephen's legs.

"What is this 'wade'?"

"It means walking in the shallow water."

"Ah. Barely getting one's feet wet."

"Yes."

"I would not care much for wading. When I do something, I must do it all the way."

"Like walking the wire," she said.

"Yes. I must do all of it and I must be the best. And I am that way in love, Juliana. When I love, I must love you completely, and it must be the best."

"Stephen, I—" She made little swimming motions with her hands.

"I know. You cannot be sure yet. But I want you to know that when you are sure, I will be waiting for you."

Did she love him enough? Was love a trembling inside when a man kissed strawberry juice off your chin? Was it the sense of pleasure she felt when she saw Stephen sitting at the Andrassy dinner table, completely at ease with her family? Was it the tender longing for him that she felt when they were apart, and was it the peaceful, exhausted sense of completion she felt after their lovemaking? Was it all of these things or none of them? Would what she felt for Stephen be strong enough to endure through everything she would have to endure if she were his wife?

"Why are we sitting here?" she asked, blinking her eyes against the sudden piercing sunbeam that managed to penetrate the leaves above.

Stephen wrapped his arms around her and kissed her lingeringly on the corner of her mouth.

"Because we fell—in the water and in love. Come on, my little water nymph," and he kept his arms around her as he pulled her to a standing position. They stood holding each other for a long time, the water eddying around their ankles.

"I almost forgot," Stephen said suddenly. He released her and reached into a shirt pocket. "I have brought you something, so you won't forget me and what you're supposed to be thinking about."

"I would never forget—" Julie began, and then she saw the tiny gold star twinkling in the palm of his hand.

"Here, let me fasten it around your neck," he said.

"Let me see it first," she breathed, her fingers capturing it as it dangled on its chain. It was a tiny five-pointed star, with a diamond tipping one of its points. It was dainty and lovely and, to Julie's mind, an utterly extravagant gesture.

"I can't accept this," she said slowly.

"Of course you can." Stephen reached around her neck and clasped the chain. The chain was so long that the star dangled in the hollow between her breasts. She looked down at it and touched the diamond experimentally.

"It's beautiful," she said.

"It has special significance," Stephen said. "Remember, I told you that my destiny was to touch the stars. In asking you to share my life, I am asking you to touch the stars, too."

"I don't know what to say. I don't know what to think." She lifted her wide, dark eyes to his.

"I think we'd better get out of this water. So I won't get cold feet," Stephen said, and they smiled at his joke as Stephen climbed up on the nearest rock and pulled Julie after him. She instinctively reached for the little gold star; she had a feeling that she was going to be reaching for it often in the next few months.

"What is that sticking out of your back pocket?" Stephen asked curiously.

"Oh, my gosh—it's the mail!" Julie withdrew several soggy envelopes, and Stephen grinned.

"I hope they are nothing important."

"It doesn't look like it. Just a circular from the Lion and Lamb Grocery, something addressed to 'Boxholder,' and a postcard for Nonna." Julie spread the waterlogged mail out on a rock that was more sunny than most, so that it could dry.

They ate greedily, stretched out on the flat rock with their feet touching, their hands meeting as often as possible, and their lips touching, too, from time to time. Their voices were murmurs; they said things that no one else would understand, and the light in their eyes flared and sparked and danced in willing intimacy.

When it was time for them to go, Julie gathered the dry mail and Stephen folded up the tablecloth. They spared one last glance for their quiet glade.

"I will always remember this spot," Stephen said fondly. "Perhaps one day we will return here with our children and show them the place where you and I first became friends."

"Maybe," Julie hedged as her fingers sought the star on the chain around her neck, but she didn't know yet. She just didn't know.

THERE WERE NO SAD GOODBYES. Between Julie and Stephen there was only a gentle leave-taking the night before, and it was only slightly different from their other leave-takings. Neither of them wanted to remember the other in sadness. Julie had known too much sadness in her life already.

"You have much to think about, Juliana, while we are apart. I will be thinking of you, too, every day. When can I expect an answer, my dearest? When will you tell me if you will marry me?"

"At Christmas," Julie said, because they were all going to gather in Venice for the winter holidays. "I will let you know then."

And Stephen knew well enough not to push her, because such a decision was not easy for her, and because he did not want to disturb the fragile peace she had made with herself. He would wait for her with longing, but he *would* wait for her, and he would hope that when they met again, their meeting would be a true celebration. He would wish for it with all his heart.

BACK IN VENICE, Julie plunged into work at the gym. Molly, her pupil with the broken leg, was still ailing. Worse, she seemed to have lost interest in gymnastics.

"See my pictures?" Molly said on the day when Julie stopped by her house to visit her. "I've taken up oil painting. I'm pretty good, too."

"We were at our wit's end to keep Molly occupied," Molly's mother said from the doorway of her room. "Finally, I got her some paints, and she plunged right in."

"Your paintings are very good," Julie said, turning slowly so that she could take them all in. Paintings graced the walls and were propped up on Molly's dresser. Some occupied the chair, and more were strung along the baseboards.

"Molly's always been a very talented artist," her mother explained.

"But I never had time to paint before. Guess what, Julie, I'm entering some of my work in the city recreation department's show. I might even win a prize!"

Molly was proud of her paintings, and Julie was happy for her. Still, it was with a feeling of foreboding that she left Molly's house. Her student hadn't mentioned gymnastics once during her whole visit.

At the gym Julie found herself at loose ends without Molly to coach. Working there simply wasn't fun anymore. Her boss put her to work with a preschooler class, but Julie found teaching four-year-olds how to do proper somersaults less than inspiring.

Life at home was difficult, too. Nonna had grown used to having Sam and Eric and Mickey and Tonia around. She missed them, and she expected Julie to spend more time with her than Julie wanted to.

Julie came home at night to find Nonna playing WROK 103, the local rock station, at full blast. The first thing Julie would do upon entering the house was turn the volume down. Nonna would invariably turn it up again.

"I got used to it being loud when Sam and Eric played their music," Nonna told her. "I like it that way."

Reasoning that Nonna might be getting hard of hearing, Julie went into her room and shut the door, which made Nonna irritable.

"Carol and I used to sit and crochet together," Nonna said petulantly when Julie emerged later. "Maybe I could teach you to crochet. Would you like to learn?"

But Julie crocheted like a person with six thumbs, and she finally gave it up. Before she had the good sense to throw in the towel, or rather the crochet hook, Julie thought she'd go mad with the utter perverseness of the little loops of yarn and with the bone-shaking volume of Nonna's rock music as they worked. Julie would have spent more time at the gym, but there was nothing at the gym to keep her there.

Carol's name crept into the conversation at odd times. It was, "Carol used to heat the butter and the milk together when she mashed the potatoes, not throw it all in at once like you do," or "Carol used to sit down and watch the *Today* show with me every morning, and we sure had some good laughs over that funny Willard Scott." Julie bore such gibes with outward fortitude, but inwardly she despaired. She was doing the best she could for Nonna, and it wasn't enough anymore.

Julie missed Stephen. She hadn't dreamed that it was possible to miss Stephen so much: his blue eyes, sparkling at her in the morning before the troupe set out across the meadow to practice, his feather-light touch at the back of her neck, under her hair; his yellow hair, so different from the dark Andrassy hair, gleaming with the light upon it. After living in the same house with Stephen for so long, Julie kept expecting him to round a corner or to come, laughing, in the front door. At such times, the gold star between her breasts hung like a dead weight, reminding her of nothing so much as Stephen's absence. At night she wrapped her arms around herself in her loneliness, trying to relive every precious moment they had spent together.

Stephen telephoned her. He said he couldn't help it—he had to speak to her.

He never pressured her about marriage. He confined his conversation to general things. He told her how practice on the wire was going, and he relayed the funny things Mickey and Tonia had said. He gave her reports on Carol's efforts at canning green beans and reported to her what new steamy novel Eva was currently reading. He was her link to the family she loved.

Before they hung up, Stephen would always say, "I love you, my Juliana," and she would reply with a heartfelt, "I love you, too." Yet nothing was resolved.

Julie went for long walks in the neighborhood after dark, pondering the inevitable question, *What kind of life would we have together?*

Stephen was undoubtedly good husband material. He had proven himself to be kind, caring and considerate. He loved her. He was good with children. He could provide well for her. He liked her family and, in fact, considered himself already a member of it.

But he walked the wire.

What good would it do to have a kind, caring, considerate, loving husband who loved their children and provided for all of them well, if he could fall from the wire at any time and die? It was a harsh question to ask herself. But it had to be asked.

And she asked it over and over and over again.

Paul called one evening after Julie had had a particularly depressing day at the gym, and Nonna, who answered the phone, responded with more animation than Julie had seen her display since they left the farm.

"Mickey lost a front tooth? His first one! You must make sure that the tooth fairy leaves him a dollar, not a quarter! And Eric has a new girlfriend? What is her name?"

This went on for half an hour before Nonna handed the telephone to Julie and wandered pensively to her bedroom, looking as though she'd lost her best friend.

"Paul?"

"Julie! How's my favorite cousin?"

"Fair to middling," Julie said.

"That's not good enough. Say, what's happened to you and Nonna? You both sound a little down."

"I've had bad news at work, Paul. My gymnast, the one who was Olympic material, has decided to give up gymnastics."

"How sad for you! I know you had great hopes for her."

"She's become more interested in art and boys, not necessarily in that order. Without Molly, I'm going to be very bored."

"That's a shame."

"I know." Julie sighed glumly.

"Julie, how's Nonna?"

Julie glanced to see if Nonna's bedroom door was closed. It was.

"She seems—oh, somehow, sad since we got back from the farm. I think she misses having so many people around. It's lonely in our house with me gone all day."

"That's what I wanted to talk to you about. There's no reason for you to feel that you have to be the only one to take care of Nonna, Julie. You need to make a life for yourself. I know you feel responsible for the accident and for her being alone, but I think Stephen helped us to see that none of us was to blame for the accident. Carol and I want to help. We enjoyed having Nonna here this summer—she was great company for Carol. And Carol's a registered nurse, so she can manage Nonna's medication and doctor's appointments. If she wants to, Nonna can come and live with us."

"*Live* with you?"

"Sure. We have lots of room, and once the performing troupe leaves, it's going to be much too quiet around this big house."

"Have you spoken to Nonna about this?"

"I wanted to check with you first to make sure I wouldn't be stepping on your toes."

"Why no, I—"

"And another thing, Julie. If Nonna were with us, it would leave you free to marry Stephen. It's an open secret within the family that you love each other."

"There are other considerations, Paul," Julie said, feeling faintly embarrassed, although she didn't know why.

"Yeah, but the guy's crazy about you. You're crazy about him. Nothing else is as important as those two facts."

"I'd live in fear for him," Julie said faintly, her heart in her throat. "I wouldn't be able to stand it when he was on the wire."

"You managed all right at Tallulah Gorge. After that, everything's got to be easy. Hey, listen, kid. Did your big cousin Paul ever give you bad advice?"

Julie smiled into the phone. "Once you told me no one would ever know if we ate two big packages of marshmallow-cream cookies. And they knew all right, because I was sick to my stomach all night."

Paul laughed heartily. Then he became serious.

"Marshmallow-cream cookies aside, I know I'm giving you good advice now. Marry Stephen, Julie. Go for it!"

Julie sighed. "I'm still thinking about it, Paul. Do you want to talk to Nonna now? To ask her to come and live with you?"

"Carol wants to ask her herself. Put Nonna on, and I'll go get Carol."

Paul set the phone down with a clatter, and Julie called Nonna.

"Come live with you at the farm?" Nonna said when Carol extended her invitation. Nonna's eyes sparkled like two shiny gray buttons behind her glasses.

Julie stood in the background, fidgeting. She was beginning to have no doubt that Nonna would say yes to Carol's invitation. Nonna missed having a big family around her; she would thrive at the farm.

"Guess what," Nonna said excitedly after she had hung up. "Paul and Carol want me to come live with them, and Carol says they will even get me my own telephone!"

"That's wonderful," Julie said, beginning to feel depressed. She had devoted her life to her grandmother for so long that she was beginning to feel as though someone had suddenly pulled a rug out from under her. She'd never had to live alone before.

Nonna sensed Julie's darkening mood.

"You don't mind, do you, Julie? You don't mind if I live with Paul and Carol for a while? It wouldn't have to be permanent. Maybe I could just stay with them for six months or so."

But Julie knew that Nonna would settle into Paul and Carol's household with little effort, just as she had before. And Nonna was lonely living with Julie; that was obvious.

"No, Nonna, I don't mind. I'll miss you very much, but I know you like having a family around you." And because Julie didn't trust herself to say anything more, she fled to the backyard, where she adjusted and readjusted the hummingbird feeder and tried to fathom what repercussions Nonna's leaving would have on her life.

Without Nonna to care for, Julie would be free. Free! She would be free, for the first time in her adult life, to do exactly what she wanted to do.

The thought was liberating. It was also frightening.

LATE THAT NIGHT, Julie lay in bed, staring into the darkness and despairing of ever falling asleep. Her agonized soul-searching threatened to take over every minute of her life, giving her no peace. True, she had until Christmas to make up her mind about Stephen, and it was only mid-September. But how could she live with this painful indecision for another three months?

She heard a floorboard squeak in Nonna's room, and she glanced at the red numerals of her bedside digital clock. It was after two in the morning. Nonna should be asleep at this hour. Alarmed, Julie slipped out of bed and opened her bedroom door.

The door to Nonna's room sat slightly ajar, and Julie tiptoed across the hall.

"Nonna?"

Nonna, sitting up in bed, peered over her spectacles with a small smile.

"Come in, Julie. You are awake so late."

"I—I couldn't sleep. What's wrong, Nonna? You're not feeling sick I hope?"

Nonna shook her head, and her long gray hair, the color of steel wool, rustled against the pillow case. "I feel very well. I don't seem to need as much sleep as I used to, that's all. When I can't sleep, I get out my photo album. It is full of so many happy things to remember."

Julie looked down and saw that Nonna had her album open to a page with pictures of Grandfather Anton. She sat down on the bed next to Nonna, sharing the funnel of light from the lamp.

"Come closer, Julie," Nonna said companionably. "Here is your grandfather. Wasn't he a handsome man?"

The picture to which Nonna pointed was of Grandfather Anton before he had left the old country. The photo had faded with age, but nevertheless Julie detected a bright adventurous gleam in Grandfather's eyes. In youth, as in maturity, he was a compact, vigorous man who had a full head of crisp curly hair, dark in this picture instead of white as Julie remembered it. In the photo, he gripped a balancing pole in his hands and was about to step out onto a cable.

"This was taken when the Amazing Andrassys were performing with a circus in Vienna. A lovely city, Vienna. That was before the second World War, of course.'' Nonna straightened the picture on its photo hinge and stared at it reminiscently.

"You were never a wire walker, Nonna," Julie said curiously. "Why is that?"

"I didn't have a feel for it. As you know, my family were trapeze artists, and I was a flyer myself when I was young. That's how your grandfather and I met, when his family joined the circus my family owned. Anton was so dashing—I'd never met anyone like him. He swept me off my feet, and that's saying a lot, Julie, because I was already flying high with our family trapeze act!" Nonna chuckled and turned the page.

"You see," she went on, "here is my Anton as he looked when I met him." She caressed a large photo with one wrinkled, papery finger.

The picture showed Grandfather Anton as a very young man with a luxuriant handlebar mustache, standing at the center of a group of caped performers. In the background of the sepia-toned picture, Julie saw a circus tent with flags flying in the wind.

"Anton was only one of five brothers, but he was clearly the star of their act. Oh, no one could hold a candle to him. I loved him the minute I saw him, and I loved him always."

"Was it love at first sight?"

"It was something like that."

"I've never believed in love at first sight," Julie said thoughtfully. "To me, love seems to be something that grows along with the two people involved."

Nonna smiled. "Well, maybe I should call it fascination at first sight. Whatever it was, it was strong enough to let me know that I must marry him, no matter what. And our love did grow. Every day of our lives together.''

"Nonna, didn't you ever think about—" Julie's voice broke and she couldn't continue.

Nonna laid a hand gently on Julie's knee. "What is it, Julie? Don't be afraid to talk to me."

Julie gazed into Nonna's bright eyes, so warm and caring.

"Before you married Grandfather, didn't you ever think about his falling?" she blurted out.

"Oh, yes. Of course." Nonna paused for a moment, sizing up Julie's intent. Then she spoke quietly and understandingly. "In fact, I thought about it quite a bit before we became engaged."

"And you married him, anyway," Julie whispered.

"Yes, I married him, anyway. Naturally I was used to the idea of accidents in the circus. As a family of trapeze artists, we had plenty of our own, but we used a net when we performed. When I learned about this crazy unwritten code of wire walkers that says they must not use a net, I was shocked. Only an insane person would do that, I thought. But your grandfather was so levelheaded and so clever that he convinced me that if anyone could survive such an occupation, he could. And he did, for a long time."

"I never heard you complain about Grandfather's being on the high wire. And you gave all three of your sons to the wire, too."

"Julie," Nonna said with an upward tilt of her chin. "We are a Hungarian circus family. We are proud of our tradition."

"I'm so afraid," Julie murmured, "so afraid for all of them." She looked down, only to see the gold-star pendant Stephen had given her hanging outside her nightgown. The single diamond seemed to droop from one of the points of the star like an unshed tear.

"I could have been afraid for my husband and my sons. In fact, many times I *was* afraid. But how silly it would have been to let my fear rule my life. I had three sons. My oldest son, Mihaly, was killed on a sidewalk by a runaway car shortly after we came to the United States. It was a tragedy, but it makes a point—life is full of danger for everyone, not just wire walkers. And the wire act is what the new Amazing Andrassys troupe wants to do. It is what they were born to do."

"Everyone thought I was born to walk the wire, too."

"You have made your choice, and the others respect that. They have made their choice, also."

"Yes. And now I must make another choice." Julie lifted troubled eyes to Nonna's.

"Stephen?"

Julie nodded.

"Do you love him, child?"

"I love him, Nonna. I love him with all my heart. And he wants me to marry him."

"Stephen loves you, too. I have seen it in his eyes."

"Oh, Nonna, what am I going to do? I came back to Venice to think it over, but I can't think because I miss him so much. I keep turning Stephen's marriage proposal over and over in my mind, and there's no easy answer. I keep thinking, what if he falls? What if we get married and he falls from the wire, and there goes our life together! It's not a happy prospect."

"Julie, I had the same thoughts before I married your grandfather. What if he fell? Well, we had almost fifty wonderful years together. If I had followed my head instead of my heart, I would not have married Anton Andrassy. And I would have missed out on the fifty happiest years of my life. I would have missed out on my three sons, Mihaly, Sandor and Béla. Would I have been better off for not marrying Anton? No!''

"Then the question is, would I be better off for not marrying Stephen?''

"And what is the answer?''

"The answer is that I love him.''

"And loving him as you do, would you rather live without him?''

"I can't live without him," Julie said helplessly.

"Then, Julie, that is your answer," Nonna replied softly.

Chapter Fourteen

Julie ran through the corridor beneath the stands of the Louisiana Superdome, searching for the Andrassy dressing room. She'd been here before, of course; she was familiar with the layout. But the man at the door must have given her the wrong directions because she couldn't find the room.

The crowd of Shriners was filling the stands; the hubbub echoed off the walls of the corridor. A man wearing a hardhat and carrying a roll of electrical tape was walking in the opposite direction. Julie stopped him.

"Please, do you know where the Amazing Andrassys are dressing?"

"That way," he told her, jerking a thumb over his shoulder. She had been running in the right direction after all.

"Thank you," she remembered to call hurriedly as she rushed on.

It was almost time for the performance. Julie's heart raced beneath the neat brown suit she wore, and her hands were clenched so tightly that her fingernails dug into her sweaty palms. But she had to find Stephen.

She couldn't let him go up on the wire without telling him what she had traveled so far to tell him.

After last night's late talk with Nonna, Julie had hurried to the gym early in the morning and resigned from her coaching job.

Her boss had been dismayed.

"But your students! What will they do without you?" He was clearly upset to be losing her.

"Anyone can teach somersaults to four-year-olds," Julie soothed. "You'll find someone to do what I'm doing without any trouble at all."

"In one week I lose my best student and my best teacher! Julie, what can I do to convince you to stay?"

"Nothing," Julie insisted firmly, and she had cleaned out her locker and walked out of the gym without a backward glance. She had loved her job, but she was going to open a new chapter in her life. There could be no looking back.

Nonna had been aglow with satisfaction when Julie arrived back from the gym that morning.

"I called a lady named Patrice at my favorite airline; I've talked with her before. She got you on a direct flight to New Orleans today. Isn't that wonderful?"

"I always knew your hobby would come in handy someday, Nonna," Julie said with a smile.

"Oh, you don't know the half of it," Nonna said, pressing a card into Julie's hand.

"What is it?" Julie asked, turning it over.

"Spend your honeymoon in beautiful Myrtle Beach!" exhorted the postcard, which Julie recognized immediately as the one that had been in her back pocket when she had fallen into the stream during her farewell picnic with Stephen.

"Apparently I got this card from one of the 800 numbers I called," Nonna said with an embarrassed shrug. "This company is giving away free weekends at their condominium. See, the condominium is called Sandlapper Seas. All you have to do is listen to a short sales talk from one of their friendly vacation representatives, and they give you the rest of the weekend to enjoy the beach."

"Oh, Nonna," Julie said, envisioning a horrendous, inescapable, nonstop sales spiel in a boiler-room atmosphere.

"Well, I thought a honeymoon at the beach would make a good wedding present," Nonna said sheepishly.

Julie stuffed the postcard in her purse and hugged Nonna goodbye.

"Take your medicine on time. I've laid the pills out for you in sequence. And Mrs. Sims next door is going to look in on you regularly until Paul and Carol come this weekend to take you to the farm."

"Don't worry about me," Nonna said. "I just got a new 800-number directory in the mail. It will give me plenty to do until I leave for the farm." She waved cheerfully as Julie backed her car out of the driveway.

Julie's flight to New Orleans had been uneventful, but she had thought she'd never get there. And now she worried that, after all her effort, she wouldn't be in time to see Stephen. A distracted glance at her watch told her that it was only a few minutes until the performance began.

"Careful, Susan, don't step on the edge of your cape!" said Eva's sharp, unmistakable voice, and Julie peered in an open door to see Eva straightening Susan's satin cloak so that it hung correctly.

Eva and Susan looked up at the same time.

"*Julie!*" they exclaimed simultaneously.

"Yes, it's really me," she answered with a grin. She was hugged immediately by both cousins, and Susan, her brown eyes heavily made up for the performance, looked confused as she asked anxiously, "Why are you here? Is anything wrong?"

Julie, now that she had found them, relaxed a bit. "No," she said. "Everything is right. I don't have time to explain now, but I must speak with Stephen. Where is he?"

"In the dressing room next door, I think. Oh, Julie, I'm so glad you're here!" Eva said. "And if you're here for the reason that I think you're here, I couldn't be happier." She turned Julie around and gave her a little push out the door. "Go find Stephen. Hurry!"

"Albert, where's my list?" Stephen's voice said, and Julie dropped the hand with which she had been about to knock on the closed dressing room door and turned to see Stephen walking toward her in the corridor. He was wearing a dazzling white leotard, and a white cape sparkling with silver sequins swung from his shoulders. She had never seen him looking handsomer.

His head snapped up in a double take when he saw her standing so quietly outside his dressing room, and then he handed Albert the clipboard he was carrying. It couldn't be—but it was! She was here! As though in a daze, he began to move toward her, slowly at first and then faster, until the distance between them melted into nothing. Julie saw the gleam of tears in his eyes before he enfolded her in an embrace both gentle and fierce.

"Juliana," he whispered as if he couldn't believe it. "Juliana."

The strength of his arms all but crushed the breath from her lungs, but it didn't matter; it didn't matter at all. Tears streamed down her face, tears of joy, because she knew he had understood as soon as he'd seen her why she had come, why she hadn't been able to stay away, why she would never be able to stay away.

"Your cape," she said weakly into his shiny hair. "I'm getting tears all over it."

"As if I care! Oh, Juliana, it is so wonderful to see you!" He held her at arm's length, his blue eyes bright with happiness. Then, as though he couldn't bear for her to be so far away from him, he wrapped his arms around her and smothered her face in his shoulder.

They had both forgotten Albert, who was standing in the background trying not to look as interested as he obviously was in these proceedings. But finally Albert cleared his throat.

"Stephen," he said tentatively, "the crew from the television station is here. They were going to film the last few minutes of preparation before we go on the wire." A man carrying a camera edged closer, but Julie and Stephen seemed not to notice. Stephen was gazing down at her, his eyes devouring the sight of her long dark hair tumbling loose around her shoulders, her eyes so dark and glowing, her slightly parted and trembling lips.

"Dearest—"

"Sh," she said. "I have come a long way to say it, and I want to be the one. Let's get married, Stephen. Soon."

The television camera continued to roll, but Julie wasn't conscious of the camera or the crew from the

TV station. All she was conscious of was Stephen, here in her arms—Stephen, whom she loved and whom she would always love.

Stephen laughed happily and swung her around, lifting her feet clear off the floor.

"I thought I would have to wait until Christmas to find out your answer," he said in wonder.

"I couldn't wait."

"Neither can I." And cupping her face between his hands, Stephen kissed her gently on the lips.

"Is this a marriage proposal I have just heard?" asked a perplexed reporter from the TV station, delighted but unwilling to believe that she had unwittingly uncovered a human-interest scoop for the nightly news program.

"Yes," Stephen said, refusing to look anywhere but into Julie's eyes.

"Is that right, Ms., um, Ms.?"

"Andrassy," Julie supplied, unable to pull her eyes away from Stephen's face.

"But—your name is Andrassy, and you're going to marry an Andrassy, so—" But no one seemed willing to explain this peculiarity, and then there was no time for anyone to say anything more. In the arena, the band galloped into a lively rendition of a Strauss waltz, and the swirl of music seemed to awaken Stephen.

"The performance," he said to Julie. "It is time. Will you be all right?" His eyes plumbed the depths of hers, and with confidence she nodded.

"Yes, Stephen. I'll always be all right."

He smiled down at her, and after one last brief kiss on her forehead, he became all business.

"Albert, my clipboard, please," he said. Albert handed it to him.

Stephen knocked on the closed doors to the dressing rooms. "Everyone out in the hall," he called.

They rushed out of the dressing rooms, and Eva and Susan threw Julie long, curious looks. But when they saw the expression on her face, both cousins burst into smiles. Julie saw Eva elbow Susan in the ribs as if to say, "I told you so."

Without further ado, the troupe lined up for inspection.

Stephen stepped forward and cleared his throat. As Grandfather Anton had done, he planned to speak encouragingly to them before every performance. Julie stayed in the background, trying to be as little distraction as possible at such a crucial time.

Stephen said, "Many people have turned out to rejoice with us about our return to the wire. We have practiced long and hard. We have every reason to find strength in our own courage. Let us all give the best performance of our careers on this very special night."

"Is everyone ready?" Albert asked.

"Yes!" they replied in unison.

"A kiss for luck," Stephen said suddenly, and taking Julie's hand, he pulled her from her place in the shadows. His arms opened to surround her, and for one brief moment he held her so close that Julie heard his heart beating steadily in his chest. It was exactly the reassurance she needed.

Then he released her, but not before she whispered so that only he could hear, "Touch the stars, my darling." It was what she would say to him every time he took leave of her to walk the wire.

Stephen assumed his place at the head of the line. The five performing Andrassys straightened their shoulders and thrust out their chests.

The brass band finished playing the waltz, and then there was silence as an announcer's voice reverberated through the arena.

"And now, the moment you have all been waiting for, the return of the Amazing Andrassys to the high wire!" The crowd cheered; then the announcer said in a more somber tone, "The Andrassy family would like you to know that they dedicate this return performance to the members of their family who died in a fall from the wire in this arena eight years ago."

The short silence following this announcement was respectful, and then the announcer said, "We bring to you the wonderful, the marvelous, the Amazing Andrassys!" The band struck up a lively march, and the Amazing Andrassys, gleaming in their white satin and silver sequins, began to stride smartly forward in time to the music.

Julie watched with pride as the members of the troupe moved as one into the arena, their motions beautifully synchronized. They were her family, and it was Stephen who had brought them back to the calling that was their tradition—Stephen, whom she had found it so difficult to trust, Stephen, whom she loved and would love forever, no matter what.

Heads held high, arms curved gracefully above their heads, the Amazing Andrassys went out to meet their destiny.

Epilogue

Julie sat next to Nonna in a crowded courtroom in Atlanta, Georgia, craning her head to get a better view. There he was, right in the front row, his pale hair shining in the overhead light. A flashbulb went off, but Stephen ignored it. Julie knew that her husband's mind was on the solemn ceremony that was to follow.

It was September 17, Citizenship Day, and one of America's newest citizens was about to take the oath of allegiance to the United States. In a few moments, Stephen Martinovic-Andrassy would complete the process that would make him a naturalized citizen of his adopted country.

Because of his marriage to Julie, Stephen was eligible to become a citizen in three years rather than the five it required for applicants who had not had the good fortune to marry an American citizen. He had already taken the oral quiz that tested his knowledge of the American government and political system; this ceremony was for the purpose of formalizing his citizenship. Stephen had chosen to take his oath in Atlanta so that the whole family could attend.

"Can you see, Julie?" Nonna asked in a too-loud voice.

"Yes," Julie whispered back. "Can you?"

"No, I can't see a thing." The two rather large spectators who were blocking Nonna's view turned and glared at her.

"Here, Nonna, let's change places," suggested Susan, who was tall and was sitting behind someone short.

Julie shifted her knees aside so that Susan and Nonna could trade places.

"Is Stephen a citizen yet?" asked Mickey, who sat fidgeting beside Linda at the end of a benchful of Andrassys. All the Andrassys, even Uncle Béla, were present for this important ceremony.

"Not yet," Michael replied.

A hush fell over the big courtroom as the newly naturalized citizens raised their hands to take the solemn oath, and afterward, a judge spoke to them about the privileges and responsibilities of citizenship. Julie was uncommonly moved by the short but stirring ceremony. She couldn't help but think about the changes that had been wrought in her life during the past three years.

Julie had been practicing on the high wire with the performing troupe for the past six months. She had even begun to hope that someday she would feel enough confidence to perform with them. It had been a long struggle, but she was finally beginning to feel comfortable on the wire. Since her marriage to Stephen, and with his encouragement, she had lost much of her fear. This time, when she had gone on the wire, it had been of her own free will. It had been her choice and hers alone.

Marriage had mellowed her; her outlook was different these days. She saw the wire as part of her heritage and part of her future. She would perform with the others, she was sure of it. She already felt part of the act; for the past three years, Julie had functioned as Stephen's right hand, traveling with the troupe and helping him with the many tasks involved with training, encouraging and booking a top high-wire act.

Working together on behalf of the act had brought Stephen and Julie even closer. As husband and wife, their love grew stronger every day. Together they had found so much happiness that their contentment reached out to touch everyone in the family. Already they had known enough joy to last a lifetime, however long that lifetime happened to be. Julie would never regret marrying Stephen. Never.

"Julie, Stephen's looking around for you," Eva said, leaning across Albert. With a start, Julie realized that the ceremony was over.

Julie fought the crowd surging up the narrow aisle toward the doors, pushing her way to the front of the room where Stephen, with his usual panache, was fielding questions from the reporters who had descended upon him, eager to uncover his feelings about this, his latest accomplishment.

"Mr. Andrassy, how do you feel, now that you are a citizen of the United States?" Julie heard one reporter ask loudly as she grew near.

"Very, very happy," Stephen said. As usual, he was comfortable as the center of attention. Smiling, he turned toward a network reporter who thrust a microphone in his face.

"This is also a special anniversary for you and the Amazing Andrassys, isn't it?"

"This month is the third anniversary of the Amazing Andrassys' return to the wire after the accident in the Louisiana Superdome in 1975. It is also the third anniversary of my marriage to my lovely wife.'' His eyes sought Julie over the heads of the crowd, and when he saw her, his face brightened as only Stephen's could.

"And now what? What's next for the Amazing Andrassys?"

"Next, I hope my wife will join our act." He held out his hand, and the knot of people around Stephen shifted so that Julie could reach him to place her hand in his. He drew her close to him and slid an arm around her shoulders. "This is my wife, Juliana," he said with a proud grin.

"Mrs. Andrassy, is it true that you plan to take your place on the high wire with your husband and cousins?"

"Yes," Julie answered easily. She lifted her face to Stephen's, her lips curving into a sweet smile.

"When will that be?" the reporter urged, scribbling notes on a lined pad.

There was a long silence, and Stephen waited for her to answer. He did not know what she would say; they had never discussed an actual date for her to begin performing with the troupe. For one awful moment, he was afraid to hear her answer. But then she spoke, and he was afraid no more.

"When I am ready to touch the stars," Julie said softly as she gazed deep into his eyes, and Stephen, wearing an expression that would later be described in the resulting article in *Good Housekeeping* as "adoring," dipped his head and kissed her lingeringly on the lips.

Harlequin American Romance

COMING NEXT MONTH

#173 WELCOME THE MORNING by Bobby Hutchinson

To Charlie Cossini and her construction crew, work came first, even when the job site was in sunny Hawaii. So when surfer playboy Ben Gilmour wanted her for a playmate, he was forced to devise a plan to lure Charlie away form her hammers and lathes . . . and into his arms.

#174 THE RUNAWAY HEART by Clare Richmond

Barbara Emerson should have been suspicious of a man as elusive as private investigator Daniel McGuinn, but instead she hired him to find a missing person. Sometimes, she thought, you had to gamble on blind instinct and hope that your instincts were right.

#175 SHOOTING STAR by Barbara Bretton

To staid Bostonian Katie Powers, the advice "Be daring" was difficult to follow. Until she was stranded in a tiny Japanese village with fellow American Tom Sagan. Then the unexpected happened: over a spectacular display of fireworks, Katie fell in love.

#176 THE MALLORY TOUCH by Muriel Jensen

Randy Stanton didn't think much of Matt's famed "Midas touch." Though he brought prosperity to the quaint Oregon coastal town, whenever they were together disaster followed close behind. But try as she might to avoid him, it seemed fate had set them on some kind of bizarre collision course.

ATTRACTIVE, SPACE SAVING BOOK RACK

Display your most prized novels on this handsome and sturdy book rack. The hand-rubbed walnut finish will blend into your library decor with quiet elegance, providing a practical organizer for your favorite hard-or soft-covered books.

Only $9.95

Approximately 16" x 8" when assembled

Assembles in seconds!

To order, rush your name, address and zip code, along with a check or money order for $10.70 ($9.95 plus 75¢ postage and handling) (New York residents add appropriate sales tax), payable to *Harlequin Reader Service* to:

In the U.S.

Harlequin Reader Service
Book Rack Offer
901 Fuhrmann Blvd.
P.O. Box 1325
Buffalo, NY 14269-1325

Offer not available in Canada.

BKR-1

Don't miss a single title from this great collection. The first eight titles
have already been published. Complete and mail this coupon today to
order books you may have missed.

Harlequin Reader Service

In U.S.A.
901 Fuhrmann Blvd.
P.O. Box 1397
Buffalo, N.Y. 14140

In Canada
P.O. Box 2800
Postal Station A
5170 Yonge Street
Willowdale, Ont. M2N 6J3

Please send me the following titles from the Janet Dailey Americana
Collection. I am enclosing a check or money order for $2.75 for each
book ordered, plus 75¢ for postage and handling.

_____	ALABAMA	Dangerous Masquerade
_____	ALASKA	Northern Magic
_____	ARIZONA	Sonora Sundown
_____	ARKANSAS	Valley of the Vapours
_____	CALIFORNIA	Fire and Ice
_____	COLORADO	After the Storm
_____	CONNECTICUT	Difficult Decision
_____	DELAWARE	The Matchmakers

Number of titles checked @ $2.75 each = $_____

N.Y. RESIDENTS ADD
   APPROPRIATE SALES TAX $_____

Postage and Handling $___.75____

                       TOTAL $_____

I enclose _____

(Please send check or money order. We cannot be responsible for cash
sent through the mail.)

PLEASE PRINT

NAME _____

ADDRESS _____

CITY _____

STATE/PROV. _____

BLJD-A-1